THA TWINZ

REALLY WITH THE SHITS

BOOK 1 OF 2

BALTIMORE'S BEST SELLING AUTHOR

KAYO

THA TWINZ

REALLY WITH THE SHITS
BOOK 1 OF 2

By Kayo

ISBN-13: 9798815826434

Contact Information:
T. Top Publishing
Frienemies400887@gmail.com
IG: @theauthorkayo
FB: Frienemies Author Kayo

Cover Design:
Dynasty's Visionary Designs (Cover Me)
Facebook: www.facebook.com/dynastys.coverme
Email: covermeservice@yahoo.com

Chapter 1

Hondo grabbed his Moncler shirt and his car keys and left out the house with a big smile on his face. He had every reason to smile like he was. His other half was being released from prison today. Hondo's identical twin; Honcho, was coming off of a five-year stint for possession of a deadly weapon charge. He played the new Bandhunta Issey mixed tape and pulled off.

Hondo pulled up in front of the Division Of Corrections on Madison and Greenmount Streets, parked, rolled a big blunt of G-13 Haze and got out of the car.

When Honcho walked out the prison it was like Hondo was looking in the mirror. His brother was smiling from ear to ear. He dropped his bag and held his arms out.

"Get over here lil' bro."

"By four seconds," Hondo said and hugged his brother.

"Man, I couldn't wait to get out here to you," Honcho said and grabbed the blunt and pulled on it. "Damn this is good."

"Come on, let's go bro."

They hopped in the car, Hondo passed his brother a .45 ACP that he had under his seat.

"This what I'm talking about."

"Yeah bro, welcome home," Hondo said and brung him up to speed on all that was going on in their projects.

"Damn bro, I missed it out here," Honcho said. "Yo, go to this address for me." He handed his brother a piece of paper.

No questions asked, he put the address in the GPS and headed there.

They pulled up to the row home in West Baltimore fifteen minutes later.

"You got some money on you?"

"You know I do," he said, giving him the whole fifteen hundred dollar clip he had in his Balmain jeans. "You want me to go with you bro?"

"Naw, I'm good. I'm just going to look out for ah nigga that I was locked up with."

"Aiight."

Honcho got out the car, approached the shabby looking home and knocked.

A nice looking, brown-skin lady answered.

"How you doing?" Honcho asked.

"Fine, can I help you?"

"Are you Gooz mother?"

"Yes, I am."

"You are the one that takes care of him, and handle all his business?" he asked, pulling the money out.

"Yes, none of his so-called buddies do anything. And that no good baby mother of his, she ain't shit either.

"Yeah, neither is your son," Honcho said and pulled out the .45, causing the women's eyes to grow as big as dinner plates.

Bock! Bock! Bock!

After her body fell from the three shots to the head, he stood over top of her body and fed her some more.

Bock! Bock! Bock!

Honcho calmly walked back to the car and got in.

"Now that's what I call looking out for ah nigga," Honcho said and pulled off.

At twenty-five years old, the twins had lived a helluva life. They were born of two gangstas and raised in the projects. The six-foot stocky, handsome, smooth, brown-skin twins was fiercely loyal to one another and never played anything in opposition of each other. The brothers was a smash hit with the ladies with their deep waves and smooth talk.

They shared plenty of similarities and only those close to them could tell them apart, but they had differences. Where Hondo was reserved, Honcho was ruthless. Hondo loved basketball and could play very good, Honcho could play as well, but he loved violence.

Together they made up a deadly combination, and their childhood friends only made them deadlier.

Chapter 2

After they went shopping, Hondo took his brother to his house to clean up. They made their way over to the projects afterwards.

It was July first and the sun was relentlessly attacking the city of Baltimore. No one in Odonnell Heights Projects cared. They were outside. From one-year-olds to seventy-five-year-olds, they were all out there.

Honcho got out first, playing games, like his brother and him always did. He walked around the corner on Shipview Way.

"Hondo, where you been? You said you'd put my air conditioner in," Bird whined.

"My bad. I'll do it in a minute," he said, looking at the crowd of guys.

"What's up Hondo?"

"Aarron what's up?" he said, dapping him up.

"All ya'll dumb," a big 6'8, dark-skin, deep, slow voice said. Everyone looked at him. "That ain't even Hondo. That's my nigga Head Honcho."

Everyone looked at Honcho, who had the dumb look on his face. Then Honcho came around the corner.

"Honcho!" Bird yelled and hugged him.

"Eeyore, how the fuck you know that this was Honcho?" K asked.

"I know my niggas," Eeyore smiled.

Eeyore was a close friend of the twins. They, along with their other friend Sauce, had all grown up together out of Odonnell Heights.

"Welcome home Honcho!" everyone greeted him.

"We might as well cook out," K said.

"Yeah," Eeyore said, standing up.

"Damn Eeyore. How tall is you nigga?" Honcho asked.

"Six eight my nigg and still stealing niggas bitches," he said, making everyone laugh. True enough, Eeyore wasn't a good looker, being dark as tar with oily skin, big feet, an awkward slow, slue footed walk, with big ugly hands and a slow drawl voice, but his dick game was legendary, holding on to a thirteen-inch piece. He drove women mad; literally. Women came from all over the city looking for Eeyore. It didn't hurt that despite his look, he got to the bag in a major way, he knew how to dress, and his gun game was impeccable.

"I'm going to get Crystal's big butt ass to bring the grill out. Let's make it a celebration," K said.

Eeyore handed Bird a knot of money. "Go with Crystal to the market. And don't forget my steaks."

"I got'chu big daddy. I know what'chu like."

"Come on my niggas, let's catch up," Eeyore said, slow bopping to his house in the projects.

The three of them walked in the house.

"Damn it feel good in here."

"Welcome home my nigga."

"Thanks man, it's good to be out here."

"Fuck was you doing in there? You was always on lock up or switching jails when I was tryna get up with you."

"Eeyore, I got to beefin' with them bitch ass gang members. You know I hate them niggas."

"Damn yo," Eeyore said.

"Damn," Honcho said, "I knew I meant to tell you something bro. Guess who gang bangin' and is high up there in rank?"

"Who?"

"London."

"Fuck outta here!"

"Hell no," Eeyore said. "Ya'll god-father London or —"

"London, our god-father. I couldn't fucking believe it."

"Hold up bro," Hondo said, "that don't sound like London."

"Believe it. When I got up the Old Jail, I guess them gang niggas knew I was on the bus. They was waiting on me. So, soon as I get situated I go to the yard. Them niggas was deep as shit, but wanted to face fight. I laughed at them pussies. I ended up stabbing two of them two days later. I go to lock up. London on lock up too. He sends me a kite by this old dope fiend ass nigga telling me to chill out, he gon' make sure I'm good. The old head said to take his advice because he was a high-ranking member."

"Damn bro. London," Eeyore said.

"That still don't confirm it."

"Bro, let me finish," he said. "When I get to Cumberland, the head nigga for the compound approached me and said my god-father London said I wasn't to be fucked with and walked away. I beat his ass two months later and promised him I'd holla at his mother when I get free."

Hondo laughed. "Damn London."

"He probably been in that shit," Eeyore said. "You know how those gang niggas is. London got power like that, he "been" down with them niggas."

"You might be right Eeyore."

"I know that ain't my nigga," a guy yelled, coming down the steps fixing his pants.

A female followed close behind him. She saw the twins and yelled, "Honcho!"

"Damn bitch," the guy exclaimed. "Get my nuts off ya breath first, before you get on my man dick, damn!"

They all laughed. She rolled her eyes.

"My ma'fuckin man Sauce Walka. What's up my nigga?"

"Ain't shit my man," Sauce smiled, hugging Honcho.

"See you still working out," he said noticing Sauce's extra hulking frame.

Sauce was a regular at the gym. He loved the way the women admired his body, especially his knotted-up eight pack. Every one of his muscles was defined and his boyish face and extra boyish charm melted and broke the hearts of plenty of women.

"Umma forever work out. What's up? What we doing tonight?"

"Big cook out in the projects."

"Crystal phat ass cooking, Eeyore?"

"You know it. I sent her and Bird to the market."

"Aiight, umma drop shorty off and hit the bar. I'll be back."

"Aiight," they all said.

The welcome-home-cook-out party was in full swing three hours later. The beautiful hood chef, Crystal, was doing her thing on the massive grill, dressed in some tight, booty shorts, a half of tank top that exposed her belly button and some fresh burgundy Jordan 7s.

The kids ran around shooting one another with the lime green, orange, purple, and red water guns that Sauce brought them.

The hood chicks was dressed in little to nothing at the party, praying that someone from the group, that they named The Money Team, chose them for the night.

Sauce, Eeyore, Hondo and Honcho sat around, smoking, drinking, and telling old war stories.

A seven-year-old walked by them with a basketball.

"Lil' Corey, lemme see that rock."

"You don't know what to do with this Hondo," he said, showing off his dribbling skills.

Hondo got the ball and everyone took notice. It was like a hush went over the whole cook-out.

Hondo showed off his flawless dribbling skills. It was magical anytime Hondo touched a basketball. He took after his father with his ball skills. He played ball at Cloverdale basketball court with the best of the best and always shined amongst them with his pure jump shot and excellent ball handling skills. He also had a post-game which made him unguardable. The whole city would show up whenever Hondo played.

He passed the boy back the ball with a smile.

"Damn Hondo. Look like you got better."

"I did bro. You gotta come see me. We got a game Saturday. I told you I bought AT a house off this basketball shit."

"That's right bro. Eat."

A Mercedes AMG GTS pulled up and stole everyone's attention. The doors went up, causing a few "damn." The driver got out with a big ass .45 caliber handgun, sending all the children running to their mothers and causing the women to shield their children and duck for cover.

He walked in the direction of the twins. Honcho pulled out his gun as he approached. The guy stood damn near nose to nose with Honcho. Everyone watching held their breath.

"Fuck you looking at," the guy asked.

"Bust ya gun nigga," Honcho taunted.

The guy started smiling, and so did Honcho.

"Ya'll niggas retarded." Hondo said.

"Young London. What's up bro?"

"Ain't shit Honcho. Welcome home," he said, hugging his god-brother.

They put the guns up and told everybody everything was okay.

"What's up bro?" London Junior asked. "I'm happy you home bro."

"Yeah, I'm happy to be home."

"Let us holla at you London," Hondo said and walked away from the group. Honcho followed him.

Eeyore shook his head. He didn't like London Junior and he didn't trust him.

Sauce tapped him on the shoulder. "Easy big fella."

"What's up with ya'll?"

"What's up with your father?"

"He good Honcho, living like a king on the inside. He said he didn't get a chance to see you, but he sent word to you."

"Yeah, he did."

"Fuck this," Hondo said. "Ya father in a gang?"

London Junior paused like he was searching for an answer. "He ain't say nothing to me about being in ah gang. Why you ask that?"

"We heard some shit, that's all," Hondo said.

"Oh aiight, look. Ya'll be easy. I just came to check on ya'll. I seen on IG you was out."

"Aiight London," Honcho said. "Get up with us later."

"You already know," he said and walked away.

"Why he lying bro?"

"I don't know Hondo, but umma find out. He was acting weird as shit."

Chapter 3

Jessup Maryland...

The twins walked up to a big house that had a brand new 2017 Audi in the driveway.

"Damn AT." Honcho smiled. "You bought this house right here?"

"Yup. All off one game. A big game. I scored forty-seven that game. They gave me an extra fifty thousand dollars for being the MVP."

"That's right bro!" he yelled proudly. "I can't wait to see you play tomorrow."

"I'ma show off tomorrow for you bro," he said ringing the doorbell.

Two minutes later, a beautiful, light-brown eyes, 5'8", petite, smooth bronzed skin woman answered the door with the biggest smile on her face.

Without hesitating, she wrapped her arms around Honcho's neck and kissed his cheek.

"Nephew! Welcome home baby. Get in here," she said. She hugged and kissed Hondo. "Why you ain't use your key?"

"This is your house Auntie."

Tamera "Auntie" "AT" Huntley smiled at her nephew.

"Ya'll hungry?"

"We good, we had breakfast," Hondo said, looking around. "You fixed the house up good AT."

"I know. It's a beautiful house, but you could tell a man decorated it," she said scrunching her face up as only she and their mother could. "I had to put the queen's touch on it. I'm a queen baby."

"We know."

"AT, you be talking to London?"

"Yeah, he was here today."

"No, big London."

She sucked her teeth. "Yeah, that nigga be calling me with that weak ass game. I just sent him a package too. Why you ask baby?"

"You know anything about him being in a gang?"

"Hell no. London?" She laughed. "Where you hear that?"

"While I was in jail AT."

"He probably got them niggas on his payroll. I don't have London joining no gang. I'll be sure to ask him when he call."

"Naw, don't say nothing. I'll holla at him myself."

She shrugged her shoulders. "Okay. Ya'll come to chill with me?"

"No," they both said, pulling out their guns. They sat them on the counter.

"We gon' pop up on Momma."

"She don't know you home?" Tamera asked.

"No."

"She gon' be so happy," she said, grabbing their guns. "I'll clean these while ya'll gone."

"Aiight AT."

"Tell my sister I love her and call me."

"Okay."

They kissed their aunt and left out feeling like they were leaving their mother to go see their mother.

Fifteen minutes later they were pulling up to the Maryland Correctional Institution of Jessup for Women (MCIJW). A thorough search and thirty minutes later they were walking in the visiting room.

Hondo approached the CO's desk. "We here to see our mother," he said to the CO he had never seen before, "and she hasn't seen my twin brother in five years. She don't know I brung him either."

"And?"

"We wanna see if she know it's him and not me."

"Your mother's name?"

"Tammy Huntley," he said, noticing a glare in his eyes at the mention of his mother's name. He hated the guy already.

"You can stand over there by the bathroom and I'll seat her there, so she can't see you."

"Good lookin' out."

Honcho sat in the chair waiting for his mother to come out. She came out the splitting image of her identical twin, Tamera, she just had on prison clothes.

Tammy 'TT' Huntley smiled when she saw her son. She hugged him tightly and kissed his cheek, then took her seat.

"What's up Momma?"

"How you doing?"

"I'm fine and you?" he said, trying to hide his excitement.

"Honcho, don't make me smack the shit outta you. Where the hell is Hondo," she asked, smiling.

He stood up and waved his brother over. After their pleasantries they all took a seat.

"Nigga, I was in labor for eighteen hours with you two bad motherfuckers. I'd know ya ass, if that's all I seen. Don't play with me." Both boys smiled. "I'm glad you home baby. I heard about the dust you kicked up on the mens' side. That's my baby. Good, 'cause I stay putting my foot in these gang bitches asses in here."

They talked for a little while and then Honcho brought up London.

"You heard anything about London on this end?"

"Whispers."

"Like what Momma?"

"He getting money on that end. He takes care of a few of the gang bitches on this end."

The twins looked at each other.

"Is he in a gang?" Hondo asked.

"I heard he was. These bitches seem to love to be on his nuts. That's how I beat two of them up. They come to me talking this I'm their big sister shit. Bitch please. I don't give a fuck what London said. They looked crazy, I went to work."

Their mother, as well as their aunt were certified gangstas. They grew up in the streets and was known to bust guns over unpaid dope deal debts. Tammy and Tamera was the dope queens out Odonnell Heights and the twins' father, Clyde Pierce, was the gun seller.

Tammy's run came to and end in 1999, when she was charged with 1st degree murder. Three men stormed their project stash house and killed Clyde. Tammy was charged with killing one of those men as they tried to rob them and with no self-defense law in Maryland and no remorse shown in court, the judge gave her thirty-six years.

"I really miss ya'll."

"We miss you too Momma."

"You go up for parole in October right?"

"Yeah, but I ain't worried about that shit. Them people can kiss my ass."

"Come on Momma, we need you out here with us."

"And I wanna be there Hondo. When they let me out, I'll be there," she said, nonchalantly. "And what are your plans bad ass boy?"

"I don't know Momma."

She smacked him upside his head. "You really left prison without a plan boy?"

He shrugged.

"I should kick your ass. Aye listen, I need you two to stay out of trouble. Honcho, stop going to prison. Your brother needs you out there to watch his back. No one is gonna have your back like your brother. Ya'll here me?"

"Yeah Momma."

"Yeah."

"I'm not going back to prison."

"You better not, and you better find something to do with yourself. That seven thousand dollars per month that you get ain't shit."

"Speaking of that," Hondo began, "How do we get that money every month?"

"I been wondering the same thing. Every month, since the day you went to jail, we been getting that money."

"And you'll continue getting it. Me and your father always had a contingency plan," she said and continued to school her boys on the importance of having a contingency plan.

They said their heart-felt goodbyes two hours later and left, and as always they felt like they were leaving a piece of their heart.

Chapter 4

Saturday…

Eighty-nine degrees threatened everyone's day. But the heat was worth enduring with the show that was about to begin at Cloverdale basketball court in West Baltimore.

The bleachers didn't hold one empty spot and the gate around the court held throngs of people. There were even some kids that climbed the gate to get a glimpse of the players warming up.

Eeyore and Honcho carried the cooler inside the fence and posted up in a good spot. They could see most of the court, so that was good. The part they couldn't see, Sauce was there posted up with K, Aarron, and Ray from the hood.

"Hondo, you not playing today handsome?" a beautiful female walked up and asked.

Honcho pointed to the basketball court where Hondo was stretching. Her mouth dropped open.

"Hondo has a twin?" she asked stupidly.

"Double the fun."

"Oh my gawd," she said. "What's your name?"

"Honcho, and you?"

"Mirra," she said, licking her lips. "Hondo and Honcho."

All eyes was glued on her forty-six-inch butt as she walked away.

"I gotta ask bro what's up with shorty. Damn she thick as shit."

Hondo stretched his six-foot frame, trying to work all the kinks out. He looked around at all the supposedly best players in the city. He smiled, knowing he was ready to go ape-shit-crazy on the court. Honcho was home and he hadn't seen him on the level he was playing at. He wanted his brother to see him go off.

"Hondo! Hondo! Hondo! Hondo!

He smiled and waved at the group of half-dressed women on the bleachers.

First play of the game The Crime Stopper threw Hondo an alley-oop and Brice was silly enough to jump. Hondo dunk on him hard. The crowd went crazy.

"That's right bro! Break his fuckin' arm next time!"

"That nigga nice," Eeyore said.

They watched as Hondo put on a clinic. He crossed up everyone they put in front of him. He even broke one guy's ankle. He tried to save face by staying in the game, but it hurt too bad. He finally came out of the game.

Four minutes into the fourth quarter, Hondo dribbled over close to Eeyore and Honcho, gave his brother a look and then dunked the ball.

"Something's up," Honcho said, looking around. He knew what his brother's look meant.

Eeyore tapped his waist, forgetting he didn't have a handgun on him. Honcho looked over to Sauce. They were watching something across from them. Whatever it was, was on the same side they were on, so they couldn't see.

"Grab the cooler Honcho, hurry up."

They walked over to Sauce, K, Aarron, and Ray.

"Fuck is up?" Honcho asked.

"K caught them niggas over there pointing out Hondo."

"What niggas?" Eeyore asked.

K nodded his head in their direction. They all stared across the court at a group of four guys that stood out like sore thumbs.

Honcho strained his eyes to get a good look at the guys. "I know one of those niggas. They gang members."

"So what's up?"

"Let's go see Eeyore," Honcho said.

"I got'chall," Sauce said, putting his foot on top of the cooler.

Honcho smoothly walked over to the group, with Eeyore bopping beside him. Hondo ran off the court over to them. The game continued, with a replacement.

"What's up bro?"

"I don't know bro. I'm tryna find out," he said. "Sass what's up?"

Sass looked back and forth at the twins.

"Which one of ya'll Honcho?"

"Why, what's up?" Hondo asked.

"I got a message from ya peoples; London."

"Yo, we don't want no fuckin' messages from him. He knows how to get at us the right way."

"And it ain't with you niggas," Honcho said.

Sass' lips curled in anger. The guys behind him faces was balled up too. A few of them even clutched at their waist.

"Yo, the only reason you niggas still living is because of London," one of the guys said.

(Laughs) "Is that right? 'Cause I like to think we alive because we really with the shits," Honcho said.

Simultaneously, the twins and Eeyore turned around and looked towards their homeboys.

The gang members looked too and saw K, Aarron, Ray, and Sauce grabbing big automatic weapons out of the blue and white cooler.

"You niggas ain't no different from any other nigga in this city. You niggas bleed just like everybody else," Hondo said.

"Tell London Honcho said that… message boy."

They all walked off, knowing war was verbally declared and they were ready. More ready than the gang members thought.

Chapter 5

The next day they were sitting in Hondo's house in front of a mountain of guns. They were drooling at the mouths at the sight before them.

Tamera circled around the boys, watching them finger the deadly weapons. "That right there is a twenty-round, two-point eight-ounce, FN Five-Seven. Great gun. Won't jam up on you."

"How do you know so much about guns AT?"

"Nigga I ain't green," the twins' aunt barked on Sauce. "That right there you got sweetheart, is a nine-pound fifteen-ounce, twenty-round, Heckler and Koch MR762A1, with a sixteen point five-inch barrel."

They looked at Tamera amazed.

"Tell me about this beauty here AT."

"Well nephew, that's a Heckler Koch MP 5 K. Four-point four-pound sub-machine beauty. This one has a sound suppressor with an extended clip that holds sixty rounds. And if you look down, right there, you'll see the box of armor-piercing hollow point bullets. Get this one nephew. It'll do major damage."

"I'll take your word for it."

"Ya'll doing a lot of finger fucking, but ain't pulling no money out."

Eeyore laughed and pulled out an eleven thousand dollar stack of money and threw it to AT.

Sauce phone rung. He looked and saw it was Bird.

"Yo," he answered. She was yelling so loud that he couldn't understand what she was saying. "Bird. Bird. Bird. I can't understand what—" he sighed with her still screaming.

Eeyore's phone rung, while Sauce was trying to calm Bird down.

"Crystal, what's up?"

"Ya'll need to get out here. Three cars pulled up out here and started shooting."

"What?" Eeyore questioned, appalled at the audacity of the shooters.

"I was on the grill when the shooting started. Them cowards was shooting in the air though. It sounded worser than it really was because they hand automatics."

"I'm on my way," he said and hung up.

"Where was K, Aarron, and Ray?"

"I don't know Sauce. They been left." she said, calmer.

"Aiight, I'm on my way." Sauce hung up and looked at the twins. "Them niggas came through shooting at our peoples in the 'jects."

"Who was that?" Hondo asked.

"Bird."

"That bitch lying. Crystal said they was shooting in the air."

"Shit Eeyore, it don't matter. They slid through our spot shooting," Honcho said. "Come on. We need a car."

Ya'll be careful," AT said.

***

Later on that night, Hondo, Honcho, Eeyore, and Sauce was parked on Spaulding Avenue in West Baltimore with wild thoughts of seriously harming gang members. Not one of them was thinking about shooting in the air. They wasn't trying to scare anyone. They wanted families to gather in grief to mourn.

Honcho smiled wickedly and clicked the safety off on the Draco. He was ready.

Hondo got out the Honda Caravan and walked to the corner. Park Heights was live at midnight. He seen a group of guys standing in front of the 24 Hour Store. Some was posted up on cars, smoking, drinking, and talking shit. He got one more look and headed back to the caravan.

"Yo Eeyore, what kind of cars Crystal said they were in?" Eeyore told him. "All them shits sittin' right in front of the store."

"Let's go," Honcho said.

Hondo, Honcho, and Sauce pulled their ski-masks down. Eeyore didn't bother, he was behind the wheel on this one. He still caressed a Ruger SR40 with an extended clip. He planned to get his too.

The three of them rounded the corner and ran into three females.

"Shhh," Honcho said, putting his finger to his lips before they had the chance to scream. He smiled as they continued to creep across the street.

"Show time!" Sauce yelled and let off.

Honcho mowed three guys down instantly. Hondo caught two guys as they tried to run in the store.

Sauce locked in on his target. He recognized Sass immediately. Sass was literally running for his life.

Eeyore pulled up, got out and shot all the cars up. "Lets go."

Hondo and Honcho jumped in the caravan.

"Where is Sauce?"

"Up there." Hondo pointed up the street.

Eeyore drove up on the side of Sauce, let him get in and turned down Paton Avenue, then made a quick right down Denmore Avenue.

"Where the fuck was you going Sauce?"

"I was chasing the nigga Sass, Honcho."

"You get'em?"

"I hit'em, but when I got down to where he fell, he was gone. I don't know where the fuck he went at."

"Fuck it. We'll get'em. I know I got me four of'em."

"I bet you did. I see you lettin' that Draco go bro."

"We going back up there," Eeyore said. He didn't believe in letting up. He was Odonnell Heights' enforcer, the protector of the projects. He wasn't going for anybody shooting in his hood.

"Ain't no question," Honcho said, agreeing.

Chapter 6

**Maryland Correctional
Institution of Jessup…**

Maniac was on a mission. His face told the story. Five people asked him, "What's up," on his way to the yard. He ignored them all.

He scanned the yard, hoping he didn't come out there for nothing. He spotted who he was looking for over by the weight pit.

He could hardly contain his anger as he approached the weight pit, but he knew he had to, or risk getting hurt for being disrespectful, even though he had every right to feel how he felt.

'What's up Maniac?"

"I need to holla at London."

They looked at his face.

"For what? What's up with you?"

"Ain't shit Slimbob. I just need to holla at London."

London heard his name and stepped out of the crowd. "You want me?'

"I need to holla at'chu alone, big bro," he said, as calmly as he could muster.

London turned and pointed to Maniac.

"Yeah, he good London. You good, right Maniac?"

"Absolutely."

"He good."

London walked off away from the weight pit with Maniac following him.

"Speak ya peace young brother."

"No disrespect—"

"You starting off wrong already young brother," London interrupted. "Usually when someone says "no disrespect," they are about to disrespect you. I don't tolerate disrespect young brother," London said and meant it.

London was up in age, but he could get down and dirty with the young boys still. His gun and hand work was still respected, as well as his son's; London Junior.

"My two lor brothers was killed up Park Heights last night," he said, fighting back tears.

"I'm sorry to hear that young brother, but what does that have to do with me?" he asked, already knowing full well what it had to do with him.

"Your peoples did it," he said, trying to keep the anger out his voice, but it was hard. He wanted to kill London. "I asked around and these twins been doing a lot of shit to us and no one put a green light on them yet. Why big bro?"

"You know for sure it was my boys?"

Maniac took a deep breath. He knew London was playing games.

"You got a flat tire young brother?" London asked, closing space between them.

The other guys noticed the move and rushed up on them with their knives out.

"You good London?"

"Yeah, um good," he said, looking into Maniac's eyes. They fell back, but not too far away.

"All um saying is we've killed niggas for lesser shit than this. How come they get to shed our blood, and they remain bulletproof? That ain't proper big bro. And it's a rumor going around that they killed Gooz's mother. His mother!"

"I don't know nothing about no rumors. I will check into the situation with your little brothers. If it's true, it will get handled."

"Aiight," he said and walked off with absolutely no faith in London or his word. He knew what had to be done. *Fuck what London said, them niggas gotta go,* he thought.

***

London walked in the cell angry at the world. *Why wasn't my god-sons listening to my many warnings,* he thought. He was trying his best to save them from the same exact fate their father suffered, but they were making it hard. At the same time they were placing him in a fiery situation, by him not taking any action against them. He hated to admit it, but Maniac was 100% right; they've killed people for lesser violations.

He grabbed his cell phone out of his stash spot and dialed his son's number.

"Pops, what's up?"

"You tell me. Fuck is your brothers doing out there, son?"

"What they suppose to have done." London Junior answered. "I just came from the hospital seeing Sass. He said they went to the projects and let a few off in the air, 'cause all they seen was women and kids. You already know what bro and'em did. Brung it to their front door like Papa John's and they wasn't in the air with it. They got like six niggas right up there and it wouldn't've been seven had Sass not rolled under a truck."

"The blow back is coming my way since I'm allowing them to basically get away with murder," London Senior sighed. "Word is starting to get out about what Honcho did to Gooz's mother. I'm sure that nigga ain't chalking that one up."

"I'm sure he ain't either Pops, but bro and'em can handle themselves. So they better not be fakin'," London Junior laughed. "They said them niggas had some real artillery up there last night."

"Shit!"

"You stressin' Pops, you 'bout to come home. Fuck that shit. Let the chips fall where they lay."

"You gotta tell them to chill son."

"I'll go holla at them."

"Aiight," London Senior said, rubbing his hand over is gray hair. "You take the stuff too shorty?"

"Yeah. Seven phones. Fifty percs. Ten ounces of grass. Ten cans of brown. And Five hundred strips."

"Good, good. I'll hit you once I get my hands on the shit."

"Aiight Pops."

"Later," he said and hung up. He sighed, trying not to let the situation with the twins stress him. But on the other hand, he wouldn't have expected anything less from the twins. They were raised around and by gangstas. It's in their DNA.

Chapter 7

Two Days Later…

Honcho sat out on Eeyore's front in a lawn chair, smoking a blunt, watching the goings and comings of the busy projects.

"What's up with you Honcho?"

"Crystal what's up with you?"

"You don't answer a question with a question Honcho."

He smiled; happy to be hiding his eyesight behind his Louis Vuitton shades. Crystal was the phattest female in the projects. She was older than the rest of the young girls in the projects, at forty-three, but you couldn't tell because she aged beautifully. Crystal also didn't have any mileage. She didn't have not one body in the projects and that was rare, and everyone respected her for it… except for the young girls, who she had to put hands on multiple times for hating, back-biting, or for just talking a bunch of shit.

"Here, you wan' hit this?" She took the blunt from him without answering.

"How long you been living around here?"

"Almost five years. I'm not from here like ya'll, but I'm from here. You feel me?" she inhaled.

"Yeah, I feel you," he said, looking in the parking lot.

"You play basketball too?"

"Huh?" he said, preoccupied.

"I said do you play basketball… like Hondo?"

Honcho ignored her and watched the all black, limo-tinted Impala.

"What got you so focused?" she asked, turning around to look.

"Watch this. Keep looking at the parking lot."

Sure enough, three minutes later the car came back, this time, slow rolling by.

He eased the Glock .40 off his waist line when the car disappeared.

"Gimmie the gun," Crystal panicked.

"What?!" He yelled. "I'm airing this shit the fuck out when it come back through here."

"Honcho," she said, looking him dead in his eyes, "give me the fucking gun. That's the police. Give me—"

He gave her the gun quickly. He didn't have to be told again. "You sure?" he asked to her back as she walked towards her house. He kept his eyes glued to the parking lot. The car didn't come back the whole time Crystal was gone. As soon as she came back, the car came back. This time it stopped. They both looked at the car.

"You better be right Crystal, because if you wrong, I hope you can run fast, 'cause I'm out."

The doors opened the second the last word left his lips. A female in an expensive skirt suit got out the car with a male in a cheap suit. They both were obviously police officers; detectives. Honcho smiled.

They approached them with a look that Honcho recognized immediately.

"Good afternoon, my name is Detective Altman," the extremely beautiful female said. The light gray-eyed detective has Honcho and Crystal's attention. The skirt she wore looked like it was painted on her phat ass. "This is my partner Detective Woody."

Honcho sized Woody up. He was a pretty boy with his personality glasses and styled hair. Honcho could tell he was a cool white boy and his bad-ass black female partner was the ball buster.

"We'd like to talk to you Mr Pierce."

"Who's Mr. Pierce?"

"Let's not play games Mr. Honcho Pierce," she said, with so much malice, Honcho had to think about if he ever had a run-in with the sexy detective before.

He was sure he hadn't. He'd never forget those eyes. "So what's up? Fuck ya'll want with me?"

"We gotta ask you some questions," she said.

He looked at her, then at Cool Quiet-Ass Woody, and said, "Not while my lawyer not here."

***

His last comment earned him a trip down Central District, downtown in cuffs. He smiled to himself the whole ride. He wasn't new to the homicide floor down Central District. He was a natural, so he didn't care when they removed everything from his pockets and placed him in a small holding cell with no windows.

Four hours later they woke him up from a deep sleep and escorted him into an interrogation room, where his lawyer Connie Yarborough was seated.

"Mr. Pierce."

"Hey Connie. How you know I was here?"

"I been down here. We'll talk about that later. Let's see what they want."

Altman and Woody entered looking like a Hollywood couple. Honcho openly stared at her derriere. Ms. Yarborough kicked his feet under the table.

"Let's get right to it. It's obvious from your prison record that you hate gang members," she said and he shrugged. "Did you fight with a Ralph 'Gooz' Sanders?"

"If you got my prison record, then you know I beat the shit outta him… Literally. So "you" let's not play games."

"Okay. Fair enough," she said, clearly agitated. "When you were released from prison, where did you go first?"

"Lemme see," he said, faking like he was in deep thought. "My brother took me shopping."

"You had to think about that Mr. Pierce?"

"Not at all. I just like pissing you off."

She rolled her eyes. "What time was this Mr.Pierce?"

"I don't know."

"Where did you go shopping?"

"Towson. We went to the Louie store first. Then Lacoste, then the Michael Kors store. The last store we went in was the True Religion store, where I got this hard ass outfit I got on now. I'm lying. We went to the Apple store last and I got my iPhone. You wanna know where we went next Detective Altman?"

"Sure, why not," she said, with as much sarcasm as she could muster up.

"Well Ms. Altman. He took me to this excellent Thai restaurant in Hanover, Maryland called Little Spice, where we both had Bangkok steak with fresh Thai basil sauce, with a side order of pineapple fried rice. If you never been, you need to go. Their food good as shit."

"What time did you leave Little Spice?"

"I don't know, it was dark though."

"It's obvious you're trying to place my client somewhere. Can you ask him what it is you want to ask him, charge him or release him. I don't have time for this banter."

Woody put some photos on the table and placed them face down.

"Look at those photos Mr. Pierce."

"Detective Altman, I'll look at them. But on some real shit, I ain't flipping shit over. You do it."

Woody flipped them over. They were of a woman lying in a doorway with multiple visible gunshot wounds. The last photo showed an up close photo of the woman's face. Her head was oddly shaped from the three gun shots she took. Her head was massive.

"What are we looking at detectives?" Connie Yarborough asked.

"The work of your client. Before he went on a fun-filled day with his twin brother, he stopped by Ralph 'Gooz' Sanders' mother's house and killed her."

Honcho laughed. "I didn't do shit. Besides, from the way Detective Altman been treating me since I been in here, if ya'll was sure, I'd be in jail."

"Are you charging my client detectives?"

"No," she said. "Not yet."

"Well, this is over. Let's go Mr.Pierce." They got up to leave.

"When was the last time you been to the Park Heights area Mr. Pierce?"

Honcho smiled and kept walking out the door.

***

Connie didn't utter a word until they reached her Maserati.

"What the hell was that?" she asked.

"What?" He questioned.

"I've sat in on countless interrogations and I've never seen a detective show as much hatred as she did towards you," she said. "Tell me what's the deal between you two."

Honcho's face contorted. "I don't know what'chu talking about. Ain't shit going on with us."

"Honcho, this was personal. I could see it in her eyes. Every word you spoke, it looked like it made her sick. That was pure hatred."

"I noticed that too, but I'm telling you I don't know her. I never ever seen her before in my life."

Connie gave him the side-eye.

"I'm dead ass serious."

"Bro!"

He turned around and saw Hondo coming out of Central District with his lawyer; Ivan Bates.

"Fuck you doing down here bro?"

"Some bullshit," he said and Honcho caught on immediately.

"You got a twin huh." Connie said. "Call me if you need me Mr. Pierce."

"Later."

"Come on bro, let's get a hack," Hondo said, walking away from his lawyer.

"Stay out of trouble Hondo," Ivan Bates said.

"Aiight."

"Come on bro, we gotta get back to the 'jects. We can't be naked out here."

Chapter 8

Everyone was waiting for them when they pulled up. They got out the hack and jumped in Honcho's Cadillac CTS and pulled off. Their phones started ringing as soon as they got out of sight.

They waited until they got on the highway, rolled their windows down and tossed their iPhones out. They were comfortable after that.

"Where they grab you at?" Honcho asked.

"They grabbed me coming out Joe's bar. I already saw them though. K took my gun and ran on their asses. They wasn't thinking about him, so they ain't even chase'em."

"They got me on Big Butt Crystal's front," Honcho said. "Bro, you know a pretty detective bitch name—"

"Altman?" Hondo smiled.

"Yeah! Yeah, that's her," he said, a little too excited.

"She bad as shit, but for some reason she hate my guts. That's who got you?"

"Fuck yeah and you would've thought I fucked her daughter, got her pregnant, and got her strung out on dope." They both laughed. "She is sexy as fuck though. I wanna fuck her."

"You stupid bro. So she was on you about that shit over west?"

"Hell naw. She had some pictures of ah-niggas mother. I ain't know shit about that. I was out shopping and eating."

Shaking his head, Hondo said, "They came at me about some shit over west. Man they were fishing. They ain't have shit."

"You think the gang members put'em on us?"

"Shit bro," Hondo said, "Them bitch-ass niggas ain't above playing with the police. I don't put shit pass them niggas."

They went and picked up two brand new iPhones and went to see their aunt.

As always, she was hoping to see them and the feelings were mutual.

"I'm glad ya'll here," she said, after hugging the boys. "That was ya'll work up Park Heights the other day nephews?"

"Naw AT," they both said simultaneously, smiling.

"Ya'll lying, ya'll feet stink, and ya'll don't love Jesus," she laughed, walking in the kitchen.

They looked at the stuff in the kitchen and then at their aunt who was putting on a Kiss The Cook apron.

"What's up AT, I thought you were out of the business," Hondo said, eyeing the cookie sheet with piles of individual grams of what looked like heroin.

"Damn Auntie, what's up, put me on."

"You ain't ready for this nephew. This dope. This ain't that kiddy shit ya'll be selling it the projects."

"I know how to sell dope AT."

She looked at Honcho in disbelief. "Right now, all you know how to do is help me bag these grams up in these balloons right here, so I can drop it off on time to this CO for your mother."

"Oh aiight."

"The hustle never stops for Momma." Hondo smiled.

"It don't stop for nobody nephew. Now, umma show you how to do this shit one time. Pay attention.

***

Odonnell Heights Projects...

K was sitting outside of Eeyore's trap house smoking a blunt and talking shit with Nay Nay. She was rubbing on K's bald head.

"Lemme stop for Tawonda catch me."

"You good, Tawonda in town."

"You want me, don't you K?"

"Yeah, you know it." He smiled.

"I been knew you wanted this pussy nigga."

K laughed. "I know that pussy good," he said, gripping her phat ass.

"Stop," she giggled.

"You know you like it."

"Come on, let's go to my house."

"Nay Nay, you got nine kids. We can't fuck at your house."

"They don't be in my room K."

"I'm waiting on somebody for Eeyore. Later Nay Nay."

"Aiitght," she said and kissed his bald head.

"Lemme hit that blunt K," Bird said when she walked up. K handed her the blunt. "The twins' homeboy with the Benz is sitting in the parking lot."

"What?" K said. "You should've said that first Bird, shit."

London Junior walked right down on them. K moved his hand to his waist, not caring that he seen him.

"Hold fast killa. I came to holla at my brothers."

"You should've called them then."

London Junior looked at the women. "Relax ladies, I come in peace," He looked around the projects. "I tried calling. Neither one of their phones on."

"Too bad. I can't help you."

London Junior shook his head, smiled, and walked away.

"I don't like that boy," Bird said.

Twenty minutes later another Benz pulled up in the parking lot.

"Now that's who I'm waiting on," K said. "I'll get up with ya'll later," he said, dismissing the ladies.

"Don't forget K."

"I won't Nay Nay," he said, knocking on Eeyore's door.

"He here big fella."

The guy got out of the Benz. Eeyore waved his way. On his way up the walk another guy came up beside him and started a conversation.

They watched the exchange with their undivided attention. Eeyore wanted to conclude Sauce's business, for him, so that he could get back to the naked married woman upstairs in his bed.

With the blink of an eye, the guy pulled out a gun and shot Sauce's connect in his head. The guy threw up a gang sign and turned his gun on Eeyore and K and fired repeatedly. They took cover and returned fire. The guy fired six wild shots and retreated to the waiting getaway car.

"Fuck!" K yelled.

"Stupid as gang niggas. I'mma kill them niggas!"

"London Junior sent him," K said.

"You sure?" Eeyore asked, praying it was London Junior who was behind the shooting.

"He was just out here Eeyore, before Sauce's man showed up."

"Fuck he kill Sauce connect for?" he questioned, going in the house, followed by K.

"Is you okay Ee—" she was saying before she laid eyes on K.

"Go put some clothes on, you gotta go."

"Okay," she said and ran upstairs.

"You fuckin' Shyasia my nigga?" K asked.

"Shyasia! Lock my spot up. I'll holla at you later! Come on K," Eeyore said, knowing they had to get out of the projects asap.

***

Later on…
They pulled up to a taped off projects.

"What the fuck?"

"Facetime Eeyore," Honcho said.

He picked up immediately. "Where the fuck ya'll been?" Eeyore asked when he saw Hondo's face.

"Fuckin' with AT. Fuck is going on out the way? Where ya'll at?"

"We on our way to Mo's. I called Sauce too, he gone meet us there."

"Aiight, we'll be there soon."

"I bet it's them bitch-ass gang niggas," Honcho fumed.

Chapter 9

Mo's Seafood Restaurant...

Honcho pulled up on Albemarle Street, hoping everyone was okay. Hondo checked his .45 because Mo's was a favorite to a lot of people in the city. Honcho did the same and got out the car.

Eeyore, K and, Sauce was already sitting at the table eating when they walked in. The twins ordered food and joined their homeboys. After exchanging handshakes and dap, Eeyore got down to business.

"Fuck ya'll been doing all day?"

Hondo explained where they went at once the police let them go, but not what they were doing with AT.

"What the hell happened out the way?"

"Some pussy-ass gang member killed my connect and shot at Eeyore and K."

"Ya connect?" Honcho questioned.

"Ya'll know who it was?"

"I know the nigga Hondo. I did a state bid with him. He's a nobody; a flunky."

"Where he from K?"

"Up Barclay and Twenty-First. Ova East."

"We go up there and send'em to God... or the devil. Either way, he gettin' the fuck from here," Hondo said, making them laugh.

"Them bitches like roaches," Sauce complained. "They did do me a favor though. I get to keep the two hunnid thou' I owed my connect."

"There's more," Eeyore said.

"What," they questioned.

"London was out there, right before the other nigga showed up."

"Out the way?"

"Yeah," K said. "The nigga walked up to me, Bird, and Nay Nay asking for ya'll. That was bullshit. I think he came to see who was out there, and then sent the lil' nigga."

"I 'on't know yo," Honcho said.

"Look, we know that's ya'lls god-brother and all, but ain't no such thing as a coincident my niggas. Something ain't right with that nigga. He's a gang member, just like his father."

"We here you Eeyore. One thing at a time though. Let's handle this situation up Twenty-First and Barclay first."

"Aiight Hondo."

Their food came. They were eating until K said, "Eeyore fucking Shyasia."

Sauce choked on his lobster meat, while Hondo spit his drink out. The rest of them laughed.

"How the fuck you get her Eeyore? That woman happily married.

"She said she overheard Kia and KoKo gossiping about me at Joe's Bar. She said she was curious and wanted to see for herself."

"And you showed her?" Sauce asked.

"No. I told her it's like a gun; if I pull it out, I gotta use it. She hit me with that I'm married shit, so I told her get the fuck out my spot wasting my time. That was like a month ago. Earlier, she came to me talking 'bout she ready. And ready she was. I fucked her four times."

"You should've saw her," K said, "she could barely walk."

Four rough looking guys, with gray bandanas hanging out their back pockets walked in Mo's catching their attention.

"These niggas everywhere," K said.

"Like roaches." Sauce smiled.

They were loud and clumsy and disrespectful walking in the restaurant.

"And they drunk," Honcho said, biting into his stuffed crab cake.

Three of the guys came and sat at the table next to them.

"Where I know you from?" one of the guys asked Sauce. In response, he just smiled. "What? I said something funny?"

A tall black dude with a blue shirt approached them. The twins, Eeyore, Sauce, and K saw 'Police' exposed on the back of his blue shirt. K eased his hand out of his pants. "If ya'll continue to be loud, I'm gonna have to ask you to leave."

"Who the fuck are you?"

"Fuck who I am, you should be worried about what I am," he said and raised his shirt, exposing his badge and department issued Glock. 40.

"The motherfuckin' law," one of them said.

"Let's roll ya'll," Honcho said, easing out his chair. Everyone followed him; including the gang members. The gang member that was harassing the cashier saw his homeboys and followed them too.

They were three cars deep and the gang members was in a Chrysler van following them.

Hondo dialed Sauce's number.

"Who this?"

"This my new number, lock me in."

"Aiight. What we doing?"

"See if these idiots follow us out the way. The police should be long gone by now."

"Aiight. Umma call Eeyore and let'em know."

The guys wasn't as foolish as they thought. They turned off way before they made it to the projects.

Aarron and Ray was waiting on them when they pulled up. They walked right up to the twins.

"Yo, ya'll gotta go see ya'll god-brother," Ray said.

"Yeah man, he keep coming out here, making the hood uneasy. They already think he set the shit up earlier."

"What he say?"

"He said meet him at his mother's house."

"Aiight yo, good lookin'."

Hondo looked at his twin brother and said, "We gotta end this, bro."

"Let's see what London Junior gotta say."

"Aiight."

AT's house…

They pulled up to their aunt's house forty minutes later. Hondo rung her bell at one am. They wasn't sure what would come of this little gathering with London Junior, but they were prepared.

"Ya'll niggas need to find another chill spot. My house ain't it. He's downstairs in the cave," she fussed. "I don't know what'chall got going on, but ya'll better get it together. Ya'll brother's" AT left it at that and went back upstairs with hopes that they'd get it together.

The brothers went down to the basement, which is what AT called the cave. London Junior was smoking a blunt watching TV on AT's 72-inch flat screen. He stood up and greeted the twins.

"What's up?"

"Fuck the small talk, what's up with your people?" Honcho asked.

"Yeah man, them bitch-ass niggas coming out our way shooting in the air and killing people. Fuck is up with you? You showin' up out there right before the shit happen."

"You think I'm part of this shit? We family man!"

"So what's good?"

"Man, I got a call from pops. Listen yo, he keepin' them fuckin' niggas in line with the blow while he in there. Ya'll makin' it harder on him with the shit ya'll doing out here."

"We ain't start this shit bro"

He looked at Honcho in disbelief. "You killed ah nigga's mother the day you got out."

"That wasn't me, but if it was, he deserved that shit."

"We ain't stoppin' unless they stop."

"I'll let pops know. No more killing."

"Not yet. After we get this nigga who came out the projects today; then no more killing."

(Sighed) "Come on twins."

"Fair is fair," they said, simultaneously.

"Pops' life depending on this truce ya'll."

"They chill, we chill," Hondo voiced.

"But after we get this one nigga."

"Aiight," London Junior said, "Love ya'll man."

"We love you too."

"You think we gon' have to kill London and his father?" he asked when they got in the car.

(Laughs) "I was just thinking the same shit bro."

Chapter 10

Odonnell Heights Projects...

Two days later they were all sitting out in front of Eeyore's trap house joking, drinking, and smoking. Crystal was on the grill again, making it happen as usual. Kia, Bird, Ko Ko, and Nay Nay was hanging on to every word The Money Team spoke.

Honcho's phone rung stealing his attention. Only a few people, outside of the people that he was around now, had his new number. He stepped away from the crowd.

"Yo!" the operator was explaining the rules for the prison call when he answered. He pressed one once she was done. "Momma."

"Hey bad-ass boy. What's up with you?"

"I'm good. We good."

"You sure? You know word travels fast in here."

"Trust me Momma, we good."

"I sent London's bitch-ass a letter over there. He can act like he don't know if he want," TT said.

"Where your brother?"

"I think he went to the bathroom."

"Where ya'll at?"

"Out the way."

"Project babies forever huh?" she laughed. Honcho laughed. "Baby, when the sun sets and the stars are visible, the goddess appears."

Honcho took the phone from his ear and looked at it. *Was my mother losing her mind,* he thought.

Hondo approached him.

"Hold on Momma," he said, removing the phone from his ear. "Yo mommy talking crazy as shit."

"What she say Honcho?"

"Something about the stars and shit."

Hondo looked in his brother's eyes and said, "Honcho, tell me exactly what she said, word for word.

He thought about it, replaying their conversation in his head. "She said, '*Baby, when the stars*'... no. She said, '*Baby, when the sun sets and the stars are visible, the goddess appears*'. She buggin' bro."

"Tell her she is your sunset."

"What?" he questioned his brother.

"Just say it."

He put the phone back to his ear. "My bad Momma. Someone was calling me. What was you saying?"

"I was just saying that when the sun sets and the stars are visible, the goddess appears. That's all."

"Aww Momma," he cooed. "You are my sunset."

"I know I am baby. I love you."

"I love you too Momma." He heard his mother hang up. He looked at Hondo for answers.

Hondo looked at his confused brother. "Mommy was just saying she needs some more suboxone. It's our coded language. Stars could be anything from strips, dope, coke or pills; but sunset is specifically strips. Moon is dope. Ocean is pills. Light is gun. God is her. Goddess is Auntie. All she was saying was get some strips and get them to AT."

"Mommy is like that," he smiled.

A guy walked out the split with an angry face, dragging a female with him, looking around. The twins walked back over to their group. The guy's eyes locked on Eeyore.

"Eeyore!" Everyone faced the man. Honcho moved his hand to his waist, everyone else just smiled. "I don't want any trouble, but please keep your dick out of my wife!" He violently jerked his wife back down the split.

Everyone burst in laughter.

"Another one bites the dust," Nay Nay said.

"Damn Eeyore, you fucked Shyasia," Bird said. "You put that big dick all in her married-ass."

Honcho watched Crystal go in her house. He waited good until everyone got back into their conversations and slid off right behind her.

"Aye Crystal, lemme use your bathroom!"

She came out the kitchen, "Why you ain't use Eeyore's?"

"'Cause, I also wanted to thank you for the other day. You saved me from catching a gun case. I definitely ain't need that in my life."

"No problem. I know you ain't know what the demon-bitch car look like," she said. No words found either one of them after that and that found themselves locked into an eye staring match.

"The bathroom upstairs," she said in a voice that was even foreign to her. "Upstairs."

Honcho smiled. He walked upstairs knowing it wouldn't be easy to fuck Crystal, but he wanted her bad. She was too thick not to have a good box. He used the bathroom, washed his hands and came out. He saw Crystal in her room moving around. He smiled and walked over to her door.

Knock. Knock.

"Crystal."

"What'chu want Honcho?"

"You want me to be honest?" he asked, pushing the door open.

"I'm no child Honcho. I'm forty-three.'

"I want you."

"Why? I'm sure they told you I haven't fucked no one around here. You wanna be the first?"

"I 'on't know about all that. I am attracted to you though."

She laughed, showing off those four gold teeth.

"What's funny?" he asked, getting vexed.

"What's funny is, I'm attracted to you too… but not Hondo. That's how I tell you two apart

"I guess that is kinda crazy. But what was you waiting for me to say something"

"I'm no child Honcho, I told you that. I would've said something the other day, but the demon-bitch showed up."

"Is that right?"

"Let me see your dick?" she asked, catching him off guard.

He reached down in his Polo sweats and boxer briefs and pulled it out. She walked over to her dresser and grabbed a ruler and came back.

"Jerk your dick; get it real hard."

Honcho smiled.

"You need some help?" she asked, coming out of her leggins. She didn't have on any panties to remove. She turned around and showed her forty-seven inches around ass. "I know it don't look real, but it is."

He was rock solid. She turned around and grabbed his pole and put the ruler up against it. She nodded in approval.

"Is it big enough?"

"Eight and three quarters is perfect," she smiled and threw the ruler. She grabbed a condom, opened it and rolled it on him and pulled him, by his pole, to the bed, where she removed her tank top and red bra.

He took that as his que. She got up on the bed on all fours and he got up behind her and inserted himself inside her already gushing box.

"Aaah," she cried out. She used her face for balance as she reached behind her and opened her cheeks up. "Sh…shhh..shhh...iiitt! Shit!"

Honcho wanted her to remember is dick, so he put on a Mr. Marcus worthy performance.

"Honcho! Hon…cho! Aaagh! Damn!"

He grabbed two hand fulls of ass and started drilling her. She went crazy.

"Oh…ooo…shhit! Fu…fuck…aaaggh! Hon…Hon…Cho! I'm… squi…squirtin'! Ahhh Shit!"

And squirt she did. Her juices was everywhere and it seem like she wouldn't stop.

She collapsed on the bed out of breath. Honcho waited until she got herself together before he asked, "You okay?"

"Wooo. Never better. You ready?"

She was ready for round two. She pushed him on the bed and straddled him. Crystal just sat on it for a while, adjusting to his width and length in that position. Once she got comfortable she rode him like a professional jockey. Crystal made sure he knew his dick was good. She was very vocal.

Honcho grabbed her breast and was kneading them, driving her crazy. She brought her knees up, put her feet flat on the bed and began frog hopping on him. Her ass made a slapping sound with every downward hop. She hopped on him until she came again. Crystal soaked Honcho's crotch.

"Damn that pussy wet."

"I'm no child Honcho," she said.

Honcho rolled her over on her back, put her legs up on his shoulders and proceeded to fuck her brains out. There wasn't no way he was gonna let Crystal fuck him. Not Tammy TT Huntley's son. He was ninety percent sure everyone heard Crystal's screams outside. Forty-five minutes and three condoms later he was exhausted, but thoroughly satisfied. He showered and went outside.

Every eye was on him when he went outside.

"What?"

"You know what nigga," Sauce said. "We waiting on you to plan for tonight."

"Ya'll could've went on and filled me in. Shit."

Crystal came out twenty minutes later. That's when everyone started putting two and two together.

"Fuck is everybody looking at?" She barked. "So you nosy ma'fuckas won't be whispering and talking behind ah bitch back, yeah, me and Honcho just fucked for a whole hour and a half. And it was the best dick I ever had in my life. Now, ya'll can move on with ya life."

"Damn bro, you fucked Crystal. Damn," Hondo whispered."

"Come on yo, we gotta change for tonight," Sauce said.

"I want in," K said.

"You know the nigga, so you gotta go," Eeyore bellowed out.

"Let's get ready then."

Hondo gave his brother some dap on the low, while the women around wore envy on their face.

Chapter 11

Barclay & Worsley Street…
K jumped back in the truck with a big smile on his face, rubbing his hands together.

"What's going on out there K?"

"Honcho, it's gang member heaven on 21st Street. I seen a bunch of gang members I know."

"Let's get busy."

Sauce took his shirt off and put his tank top on his shoulders. "Ya'll know what to do.

***

21st & Barclay Street…
The corner was lit at eleven pm with a bunch of gang members. They had the music blasting and was having the time of their lives. The guy who killed Sauce's connect was sitting on someone's step, away from the crowd. He had got a fair warning from London Junior that the twins was coming for him. London Junior told him to lay low, but he wasn't ducking the twins. He wasn't scared at all.

"Mularu! You all actin' anti-social and shit. Come on over here," one of his gang sister's said.

"I'm good yo. Ya'll go-head."

"Come on nigga. You want this pussy, you better come on. Then again..." she said, letting her eyes linger on the shirtless god. "Hey handsome."

"What's up beautiful, how you?'

Mularu looked on. "This bitch really playing with me," he said, getting up off the steps.

"What's ya name?" she asked, looking at his abs.

"Buff, what's yours?"

"I'm only kidding honey. My boyfriend ready to come over here and lose his top."

"Ya'll got some weed around here?"

"Who the fuck is this?"

"Come on Mularu. He looking for some weed."

"Shut the fuck up Mary. Who you?"

"I'm Buff my nigga. I'm lookin' for some grass."

"Grass huh?" Mularu said.

"Who this cuz?"

"This cocky-ass nigga lookin' for some grass he said."

"Some grass, huh?" Sin said, "How much you got cuz?"

They was so focused on Buff, they never saw the twins and K creeping up behind them with automatic assault rifles.

Buff/Sauce pointed behind them with a scared look on his face. They all turned around. Sauce pulled his gun out and put one well placed bullet in the back of Mularu's head. He ran before his body hit the ground. The twins and K lit 21st and Barclay up like the 4th of July. Bodies were falling and scrambling everywhere.

Honcho walked around to each body, making sure they were dead with one to the head. He wasn't taking any chances.

***

**Maryland Correctional
Institution of Jessup…**

It took all of twenty-four hours for the news to travel to Jessup about the shooting and forty-eight hours for the rumors to start swirling about who was behind it.

The gang members was in an uproar about the recent events on the streets. So the lieutenant of the gang of Jessup, Slimbob, wrote a coded letter to the leader of the gang in Cumberland's Ultramax, and had just received a response. He called a meeting in the chapel with the respected gang members for various 'hoods in Baltimore. He wanted them to know what the boss said.

He walked in last, causing everyone to get quiet.

"Aiight homies listen. I wrote the old man last week about everybody's concerns."

"What he say about these bitch-ass twin niggas?"

"We gonna get to that bro," Slimbob said to Twon from 21st and Barclay. "The dues. You niggas that's catching, ya'll gonna hafta step it up. Ain't no more late fees. The family gets theirs off top. No more waiting. You try to slide it to ah outsider thinkin' we won't find out, ya ass gettin' chopped up. Flat out. Pay ya dues. We got brovas that ain't got shit. Tighten the fuck up," he said and meant it. "You niggas that got these bitches that's on some relationship shit, get'cha shit in order. This is a business. Those other niggas ain't faking. They gettin' money. We fuckin' around."

"Homie, what's up with these twin niggas? Them niggas killed my sister Mary last night. I need to let the brovas in my 'hood know what's poppin'."

"Unfortunately Twon, the old man said they aren't to be fucked with," Slimbob said, earning a bunch of sighs.

"This some bullshit!" Twon spit. "Them niggaz killed Gooz mother, my sister and some brovas and them niggas ain't greenlighted yet? Man fuck that!"

"So what you sayin' Twon?" Slimbob questioned, praying he said fuck the old man laws, so he could order his death. With the snap of his finger he would be done. "What Twon?"

"I'm just saying homie, my sister was a sister too. Maniac's two lor brothers wasn't even involved in nothing. And they violated going at the brova's mother," he said, having other reasons not known by anyone else.

"We know this. He knows it also. We don't know what the old man got planned. I know what he told me. So I'm following orders." he said. "I'm also enforcing them."

London walked in the chapel and saw them congregating. He walked over to them.

"What's up Slimbob?"

"Ain't nothing big bro. Same ole."

"I wasn't invited to the meeting?"

"I was gonna fill you in later. Plus the old man said he wrote you too."

"He did, but I still wanna be in the loop."

Slimbob nodded but he knew London would have slapped Twon, had he heard him voicing his concerns.

"Yo London, lemme holla at'chu real quick bro."

Maniac knew how it was gonna go, so he moved closer to them, just in case London was feeling froggy. He'd surely help Twon. He didn't like London anyway.

"London, me and you ain't never had no problems. I always respected you. My uncle even told me you saved his life once."

"There's a 'but' here somewhere?"

"Your god-sons. They killed my sister the other day."

(Sighs) London shook his head. The twins was making his bid hard. Then he received a very threatening message from a woman he considered his sister, Tammy TT Huntley.

"I'm sorry to hear about your lost. I am. I spoke to my god sons and they gave me their word that they'd chill unless it came to them first."

Twon was trying to hold his composure, but it was extremely hard. "My sister ain't have shit to do with what Mularu did out the projects."

"My son told me he personally approached Mularu about the severity of the situation and told him to disappear."

Twon's face contorted. He had enough. "Who the fuck ya'll think these niggas is?"

"Watch your tone young man."

"That's my sister," he said through clenched teeth and walked off.

Maniac caught up with Twon on his way out the chapel.

"What's up broski?"

"Homie, it took everything in me not to stab that nigga just now. I swear."

"I go home next week Twon. You come home a week later."

"So you with me?"

"Yeah," Maniac said, "But I'm not tryna get a green light put on me at the same time."

"I don't even give ah fuck," Twon said.

"I do. Come on homie. Revenge is justified and expected, but revenge unplanned is inexcusable. We gotta be smart and get away with this shit."

"Aiight."

"We gon' do this shit for me, you and Gooz." Maniac smiled wickedly.

"And my family," Twon said, knowing he had to kill the twins and they had to die by his hands.

Chapter 12

Sandra Altman sat at her desk, with files piled real high next to her. She knew these recent gang executions was at the hands of one gang. She also knew the twins had a hand in the murders somehow.

"Working late Altman?"

"Yes. I know there's a connection here, I'm just missing it."

"Every crime scene the witnesses say the suspects had on ski masks."

"That's not it Berrientos. The height, the build, the getaway car, the guns is always different, but I know there's a connection."

"The victims are all gang members."

"That's part of it, not all of it," she said, rubbing her hands over her long ponytail.

"Let's go eat Altman. Take a break."

"Go home to your wife Berrientos."

"Ooooh, that hurt. Alright, good night. Don't stay too late."

"I will," she said, with a sigh. "Dammit, what am I missing here?"

The captain came rushing through the door in a hurry ten minutes later.

"Hey cap."

"Altman," he said, stopping dead in his tracks. "You still here?"

"Yeah cap, I'm working on—"

"Where's Woody?" he interrupted.

"Home."

"You do the same."

"I will… eventually."

"No, now."

"You're here," she countered.

"I left my wife's anniversary gift. I just came to grab it. Now go, that's an order."

She sighed once again and reluctantly followed her bosses order.

***

BWX Lounge…

They wanted a change of scenery so they decided to go to an all white party at the club BWX. Sauce promised his boys a good crowd. The club was up Interstate 295 by BWI airport. The gangstas and bums stayed closer to the city, but they still packed their heat… just in case. They wasn't about to take London Junior's word that the gang was falling back. They were ready.

They paid for VIP and walked inside, untouched, after sliding the bouncers five blue face hundreds.

"Damn, it's nice in here," Hondo said.

"I told you."

They went in VIP, grabbed a table and waited for their drinks.

"Yo, how did you get Crystal?"

"Huh?"

"You heard me nigga," Eeyore laughed. "Oh, you gon' keep it to your chest Honcho?"

"It ain't nothing to say."

"Sauce," some ladies walked up and said in a sing-songy type of way.

"What's up ladies."

"Long time no see."

"Let me make up for that," he said, turned to his guys and said, "I'll catch up with ya'll later." He winked and stepped off.

"That's why I drove my car," Hondo said, shaking his head and that's when he saw her. "Got damn."

Eeyore and Honcho followed his gaze.

"Damn is right bro. Go get her."

Hondo didn't have to be told twice. He was watching the future Mrs. Pierce. He walked over to her and was surprised she was even sexier up close.

She was five foot eight, smooth as a baby's bottom caramel skin, soul stealing green eyes, no stomach to speak of, thick thighs, a big derriere, but not embarrassingly big and the prettiest feet he had ever laid eyes on.

"Cat got your tongue?" she asked and smiled.

"Oh gawd, the smile too?" he said. "No disrespect miss, but as bad as you are, your breath gotta stink."

She laughed, taking no offense to his comment. "I never heard that one before," she said, moved closer to him and blew her breath in his face. "Now what?"

"Your feet.

She removed her feet from her five thousand dollar Roger Vivier open toe heels and raised her leg. Hondo didn't care how much of a clown he looked like. He grabbed her foot and smelled it.

"No odor there," he said, contemplating asking her to smell her box next.

"Not even," she said, reading his mind with her face frowned up.

He chuckled. "What's your name Ms. Perfect?' he asked, holding out his hand.

She extended hers and said, "Ivyana, and yours?'

"Hondo."

"No nickname. Your real name."

"And again Hondo."

"Okay. Do you normally smell a woman's breath and her feet before you get her name?'

Hondo laughed. "No, normally I don't. But this is anything but normal. Where you from Ivyana?'

"Baltimore."

"Baltimore is small and I'm positive I've never seen you before."

"You didn't ask me where I live. You asked me where I'm from."

"Where you live?"

"DC."

"That explains it."

Eeyore and Honcho walked up.

"We hitting the dance floor bro."

"Aiight," he said, watching Ivyana.

She didn't get giddy over seeing his twin brother like most women did. She was real cool about it. That was a first for him.

"I bet you're not this quiet when you with your boys."

"I'm not," he said, at lost for words. He didn't want to mess up because he was still convinced he was standing in front of Mrs. Hondo Pierce," Let's go to my table."

"Forget who I'm with?"

"No. Naw, not at all. Where are they, so I can ask them to borrow you."

"I'm just kidding. They won't leave me. Lead the way."

Honcho and Eeyore was still on the hunt but didn't see anyone that stood out.

"This club big as shit."

"Yeah, it is," Eeyore agreed.

Twenty minutes later, Honcho noticed the girls that was with Sauce walking too fast and looking too scared.

"Get them bitches, I'm going to the bathroom," Honcho said, and hightailed it to the bathroom.

He found some guy in one of the stalls unconscious with his pockets inside out. Honcho checked for a pulse. It was faint, but it was there. He left the robbery victim and went to find Eeyore.

He found him in the corner with the two women, who looked on the verge of tears.

"Where the fuck is my homeboy?"

"Who Sauce?"

Honcho, not in the mood for games, pulled his gun out and put it to the girl's side that was closest to him. Eeyore did the same, so her homegirl wouldn't feel left out.

"Yeah bitch, Sauce."

"Sauce been left us," she cried out.

"Yeah, he went outside, saying he was going to make a call."

"He said he was coming back, but he never did, so we started working."

Honcho and Eeyore looked at one another.

"I swear, he been left us."

"What the fuck is that in the bathroom?"

"I gave'em too much and killed him."

Eeyore jammed the gun in the girl's ribs causing her to scream out in pain, but the music drowned out her noise.

"Not Sauce. A guy Sauce pointed out to us to rob."

"Wait, he knows ya'll be robbing—"

"How you think we started? He taught us to rob. We got good at it, been doing it ever since."

"We would never hurt Sauce. We love him. I swear he left us to go make a call. At least that's what he told us."

"We had plans to go with him tonight once we found a lick."

"What'chu think big fella?"

"I 'on't know. Sounds good."

"Lemme see ya'lls IDs."

Without hesitating they took them out and handed them over. Honcho took pictures of the IDs and the girls.

"Oh shit, the guy is stumbling out the bathroom," one of the girls said.

"Which way did Sauce walk?"

"Out the door," she said, ducking with her friend.

"Get the fuck outta here. If ya'll lying, we coming for you."

They nodded their heads frantically and left the club immediately.

"Fuck is wrong with Sauce?"

"Try his phone," Honcho said, looking around the club. "Come on."

"It's just ringing Honcho," he said, as they made their way to the front door.

They walked out, expecting to find Sauce entertaining some females, but that wasn't the case. They looked at the groups of white wearing party goers. Sauce's white Versace shirt was extra tight and as brolic as he was, he would be easy to spot.

Eeyore tried his phone again. No answer.

"Time to get bro."

"Ya'll looking for your homeboy? The cocky one?" the bouncer asked.

"Yeah," they both said, simultaneously.

"He walked around to the parking lot with a brown skin guy."

"You sure?"

"Positive. Like twenty minutes ago."

"Stay here, I'm going to get bro."

Honcho rushed back in the club and ran into Hondo coming on the dance floor.

"Where ya'll been at?"

"We can't find Sauce, come on?"

All three of them walked around to where the bouncer said he seen him walk. Eeyore tried his phone again, while Honcho filled his brother in on all that happened.

"Shhh," Honcho said.

All three of them heard the familiar ring of the iPhone 10.

"Call it again Eeyore."

Two minutes later they found Sauce's phone in between two parked cars. Blood was on the phone and the cars.

"Fuck! all three of them yelled.

Chapter 13

They didn't have Sauce's keys, so they had to leave his car and ride back in Hondo's Benz. On their way back, Eeyore called Central Bookings, and the hospitals; to no avail. They didn't know what to do.

"I 'on't believe this bullshit," Honcho said. "This nigga wouldn't have left with nobody without getting one of us, or went out to make a call."

"Right bro. He know what the fuck going on out here. Ya'll believed them bitches?"

"Yeah, but we got pictures of their ID's."

"We shouldn't have let that nigga talk us into going out, knowing we at war," Eeyore said. "Call London Junior. See what the fuck he gotta say."

"It's four am big fella."

"So?"

Honcho called London Junior.

"Yo," he answered out of his sleep on the fourth ring.

"Yo bro, this Honcho."

"Honcho? What time is it?"

"Four oh five," he said, looking at his Rolex Yacht Master II. "Look bro, you told me this shit was over."

"What?"

"Bro!"

"Yo, yo, yo. What's up?"

"Hit me when you get up," he said and the phone line went dead. "That nigga sleep."

"Aint shit we can do now. Let's meet up later."

They all went their separate ways, each one with hopes that Sauce would turn up okay.

***

The four days after BWX slowly crawled by for Hondo, Honcho, and Eeyore. The streets wasn't buzzing, no one was accepting or claiming responsibility. It was nerve wrecking. Even Odonnell Heights suffered. Sauce was the adrenaline of the projects, he was also the projects sole source of cocaine.

The twins fixed the cocaine problem by buying two bricks from their aunt; AT. She gladly sold her nephews the 90% pure cocaine. The junkies was happy, but the pulse of the projects was still weak.

***

A week later nothing had surfaced about Sauce. But the traffic in the projects had picked up rapidly with the new cocaine. That had worked out for the twins and Eeyore. They were getting money and their traffic brung some attention to Eeyore's dope. He was up to twenty thousand a day now in the projects.

They all stayed busy to take their minds off of the obvious.

***

Honcho watched his team run up and down Shipview. He saw his brother's all black S550 pull up. He also noticed how his brother was dressed.

"What's up bro? Louie linen. Louie shoes. Bust Down Rolly. Where you going?"

"Gotta date."

"With who? The girl you been on the phone with all week?"

Hondo just smiled.

"Do you bro. See if she got a sister."

"Aiight," he said, looking around. "What's going on out here?"

"Shit, we eatin' Just like back in the day bro."

"Eeyore went to holla at some people about Sauce."

"Hopefully something comes from that shit. We need to find Sauce."

"Hell yeah." Honcho said.

The Benz GTS pulled up grabbing their attention.

"Hopefully this nigga got something to tell us."

"Don't count on it Hondo."

London Junior walked up, styling as usual.

"Damn, ya jeans tight enough?'

"Cut it out Honcho. Aye, I came to holla at'chall."

"I hope it's good news."

"Or some news we can use."

"Yo, the gang ain't have nothing to do with Sauce. Word is ya man ah thief."

"What?" they both questioned.

"That's what I heard. It wasn't us - I mean the gang. That's my word."

Neither twin let the "us" in his statement get by, but they'd address that later.

"Who he 'pose to stole from?"

"Ain't nobody saying bro. What I did get though, was that it got something to do with two bitches."

The twins looked at each other. They let London blab about the (his) gang having nothing to do with Sauce's disappearance and he was still holding up his end of their agreement. After they assured him that they wouldn't do anything to the (his) gang, he left.

"Yo, we gotta go holla at them—"

"I already know bro. We shouldn't have let them bitches go." Honcho shook his head.

"Come on bro."

"Naw, naw. Go 'head on your date."

"Fuck that date bro."

"Hondo, go. We'll wait for you. I gotta go pick up my truck anyway. Go bro. When you get back, we'll be here. Then we'll all go."

Hondo wasn't feeling his brother's plan.

"Go bro. Keep ya phone on."

"Who you gettin' to drive the Caddy? K can't drive and Ray, and Aarron is locked up."

"Crystal driving."

"Aiight, call me."

***

Range Rover of Owings Mills...

Crystal and Honcho walked around the lot eyeing the luxury trucks. He needed Crystal's eye. Without her, he would've chosen the first one he saw.

"You know everybody saying we a couple now," she said, opening the door to the Range Rover she liked.

"You ain't the type of woman that let he say she say get to you, so what's up?"

"Nothing."

"Come on Crystal," he said, opening the back door of the Range she was inspecting. "You catching feelings?"

"Not at all. I mean, the dick amazing, but I'm straight."

"You sure?"

"Yeah," she said, closing the door. "This one here."

Honcho looked at the dark green, 4-6, fully loaded, 2018 Range Rover Velar and smiled. "Yeah," he said. He could already see himself getting hated on in traffic.

An hour later, he was pulling out the lot in his brand new truck. Crystal pulled out behind him in her gifted Cadillac CTS. She knew the projects was really gonna talk now.

***

Guilford Avenue…

The Toyota Avalon was parked on 22nd Street with the sole occupant's eyes glued on the entrance of Baltimore's main Parole & Probation building.

He knew that everyone from Baltimore that was released from prison had to report to Guilford before being assigned to their own district.

He smiled ten minutes later when he saw the guy exit the building. He tucked the .45 in his dip and got out.

The guy walked towards him. He put his head down. Ten meters away. Five. He raised his head locking eyes with the guy. The guys reaction was shocked at first.

"You ain't playing is you?" the guy smiled.

"Not at all. I'm ready to get rid of those pussy-ass twins. On the gang."

"I'm all the way in Maniac."

"Aiight Twon, it's gonna get ugly."

They shook on it and jumped in Maniacs girls car.

Chapter 14

Later on…

Honcho beat on the steering wheel of the Chrysler caravan in frustration. Eeyore just shook his head.

"Two fuckin' abandon houses!"

"Them two snake-bitches was involved the whole time," Eeyore fumed. His voice seeming like it was vibrating the whole van.

"At least ya'll got the bitches' pictures," Hondo said. "Get Bird or Nay Nay's nosy ass to post the pictures on IG and see if someone know them."

"Yeah, somebody should know them bitches if they really be in the clubs. Let's just hope they wasn't lying about their robbing hustle."

"If I catch these bitches I swear on my father's grave I'mma get'em right, watch," Honcho said, out of anger.

"We gon' get'em back bro. Let's call it a night."

"Aiight."

"Bro, um going over this bitch house. She in the 'hood, so umma call you in the morning to pull up. She too phat for me not to go over there."

"No Crystal tonight?"

(Laughs) "Naw bro. You'll see her in the morning. She thick as fuck."

"Aiight bro. Call me and be safe," Hondo said.

"Aiight bro. Later big fella."

***

Honcho pulled up on Reese Street in the Waverly Apartments aka The Nolia in a car that was driven by a fiend.

Gia was in the door waiting on him in a colorful silk robe. He could smell that she was fresh out the shower when he walked by.

"You wasn't about to let even one day go by, was you?"

"Not with all that ass, I wasn't."

"Shhh, my kids sleep."

"How many kids you got?"

"Two. Three and six. Two boys. Same baby father."

"Oh," he said, eyeing her as he sat on the couch.

"What'chu looking at Head?" she smiled."

"You know what I'm looking at."

"Boy you crazy," she giggled. "So why they call you Head? You always get head?" she asked salaciously.

Honcho laughed. "Naw Gia. Head is just the first part of my name. My whole name is Head Honcho."

"Oh, you ah boss nigga?"

"Yeah," he smiled, "a boss nigga that just so happens to love gettin' head.

"Umph," she said and dropped her robe. "You hungry?"

He looked at how phat she was standing there in her Pink boy shorts and PINK bra. She had no stomach to speak of and an ass that was Nicki Minaj worthy. She also looked like she was black and Korean. He could tell her long, jet black, silky hair was hers. Her feet was a little jacked up, but they were painted to match her bra and panties, so that made it better. Her fingernails matched too.

"Naw, I ain't hungry. You?"

"Of course," she said.

"Can I smoke this blunt in here?"

She normally didn't allow no one to smoke in her house, but Head Honcho was a boss.

"Go 'head."

He rolled up and then sparked it. She got on her knees in front of him. Before she begun, he pulled out the FNS 9mm and placed it on the couch next to him.

It seemed like the gun activated the freak in her, because she got right down to business. She pulled his Versace jeans down to his ankles and pulled his dick out of his Versace boxer briefs. Gia got familiar with it first, by playing with it, kissing the tip and pulling on it. She slapped herself in the face with it, then put her mouth on it, before making it disappear completely in her mouth. She showed that she didn't have possession of any gag reflexes. She ate him up. Gia showed off, let go, and no-handed the dick. She even threw up the peace sign, to pay homage to her favorite dirt bike rider in the city. Honcho placed his hand on her head as his toes curled in his Versace shoes.

"Damn," he said.

She was real sloppy with her fellatio and he was loving it.

"Shit. Here it come. Ugghhh."

He thought she was gonna stop, but she did no such thing. She got off her knees with the dick still in her mouth and started shaking her phat ass; still sucking the soul out of him.

Honcho came long and harder than he ever have in his twenty-five years of living. Gia took it out her mouth and let him squirt the rest on her face. When he was done, she had cum in her left eye on her nose, on her right cheek, her forehead and all over her lips.

Gia looked up at him with one eye closed and smiled.

"I'm gonna fuck the shit outta you," he vowed.

Honcho stood up, watching her, and took his clothes off. She kept her eyes glued on him.

She removed her boyshorts and bra and let them fall where she stood. Gia turned around walked to her room extra stanky.

"Damn you phat as shit," he said, shaking his head and grabbing hisself.

"Come get it then," she said, calling him with her finger.

Honcho was naked but he didn't forget to grab his gun. He sat it on the nightstand.

Gia was on the bed on her back waiting for Honcho.

"Come on Gia, ya ass is too phat to be on ya back," he said, rolling on the condom she had out for him.

She giggled and got on all fours. Honcho got behind her and entered her ocean, wet box.

"Oh my gawd boy. Shit!"

He grabbed her waist and plowed into her with force. She wasn't worried about the kids at all. She screamed with every thrust. Honcho had to keep looking back at the door to make sure the kids wasn't there.

"Fuck me Head Honcho, ohh shit," she cooed. "It hurts so good."

He felt when she came. He felt her juices gushing out on him and down his sack. She collapsed on the bed.

Honcho got on his back. She changed the condom and got on top of him.

"You ready for this ride?'

"I never ducked nothing in my life," he said.

Honcho didn't duck it, but he definitely wasn't ready. She placed his dick inside her butt and rode him. His eyes stayed glued to the door now, because she was screaming like a mad woman, going ham on the dick. She grabbed her honeydew melon size breast and massaged them. He didn't want her to wake the kids, so he grabbed her breast and pushed them up to her full lips. She caught on and began sucking her own titties. That kept her mouth busy while she rode him.

He flipped her over once she came and stayed inside of her butt and gave her the best sex of her life. She was ready to tattoo his name on her ass and she told him so.

After an hour and a half of many sexual positions, they were exhausted. Gia fell asleep with Honcho still inside of her.

Honcho woke up at seven am, put his clothes on, texted his brother and went to the bathroom. On his way out, he ran into the six-year-old. He just stood there looking at Honcho.

"What's up lil' man?"

"You tryna see me in Madden?" he asked with cold still in his eyes.

"Wash ya face and brush ya teeth first. Then I'll play you, but only 'til my ride come."

"You ain't staying?"

"Naw. Go 'head."

He was back in three minutes. He hooked the game up to the living room's TV and started the game.

"Who you picking," he asked, excitedly.

"Ravens of course."

(Laughs) "You gon' lose," he said. "Tom Brady all day."

Honcho smiled. "What's your name?"

"Lor Day Day. Big Day Day is my father."

"Oh."

"What's yours," he asked, choosing his team.

"Head Honcho."

"What type of name is that?"

"Ask ya mother," Honcho said.

Ten minutes into the game someone knocked on the door.

"Go get your mother Lor Day Day," he said, when he saw him going to the door.

Lor Day Day looked at him and then opened the door anyway and then came back to the game.

Three guys walked in. Honcho smiled and shook his head when he saw all three of them with gray bandannas and gray 993s on. *I can't shake these bitch-ass niggas,* Honcho thought. All of them stared death at Honcho.

"Where the fuck ya mother at?"

"In her room daddy."

Big Day Day looked down and saw his baby mother's bra and panties on the floor. Honcho ignored them and focused on the game. Big Day Day rushed to her room. The other two guys just mean mugged Honcho.

"Who you cuz?" one of them finally asked.

Honcho ignored him.

"What'chu hard of hearing my nigga?"

They heard some tussling in the back that caused them all to look back. Lor Day Day ran back there.

"Stop daddy!" they heard him yell.

"Go in your room Daymont!"

"No ma! Let her go daddy!"

"Take ya lor ass in your room!"

Honcho stood up. He saw Big Day Day with his hands around Gia's neck. He winked at Lor Day Day and motioned his head to his bedroom. He went in his room without fussing.

"Let me go Day Day. Me and you not together. I am a single woman."

Honcho was thinking about his promise to his god-brother. "Shit," he muttered.

He let her go and approached Honcho.

"Who you nigga? Up in here playing games with my son?"

"I'mma go outside and wait for my ride."

The two guys blocked the door. Honcho smiled.

"Let him leave ya'll," she said, knowing he was strapped. "You see he don't want no smoke. Let'em leave."

"Shut up bitch. I asked this nigga who the fuck he is."

"It don't matter who I am nigga. Gia is single. I don't gotta tell you shit."

"Nigga!"

Honcho's phone rung. He answered it.

"Yo… yeah… oh yeah… yeah… Make sure the light shining." He hung the phone up and pulled his gun out.

They all backed up some.

"I told ya'll to let'em go. Now look."

"Shut the fuck up Gia," Big Day Day said. "He ain't the only one with ah gun." He pulled out a .38 revolver.

Honcho laughed and walked out the house. He immediately saw the two guys his brother told him about on the phone.

As soon as Hondo saw his brother, he raised up off his Benz, openly carrying in both hands a sixty shot SKS with a red lazer beam attached. "What's up bro?" he asked, with his face twisted.

Everyone else spilled out the house, Gia included, but no one said anything.

"I'on't now bro, you gotta ask them that. I'm fine," he said, waving his FNS.

Hondo looked in the direction of the all gray wearing gang members and asked. "So what you say fellas, we got a problem here?"

They shook their heads.

"Thought so, bitch-ass niggas." Honcho looked back at Gia. "Aiight Gia babe. Call me."

"Bye Gia." Hondo waved the SKS.

She waved back with a big Kool-Aid smile on her face. The twins jumped in the Benz and pulled off.

Chapter 15

Friday…

Eeyore was giving packs out to his workers when the twins pulled up for the second time that morning.

"What you drop the truck off for Head Honcho?"

"Eeyore, you know I gotta give my truck some type of personality. Game system, five percent tints, TVs, twenty-sixes on the shoes and I got the grill changed. I gave'em an extra twenty to be done today."

"I hear that shit."

Bird and Nay Nay walked up.

"Eeyore, Hondo, Honcho," they both spoke. They all spoke back.

"Got some good and bad news ya'll."

"What is it Bird," Honcho asked.

"The good news is, damn near everybody on The 'Gram knew them bitches."

"Damn near every nigga who recognized them is looking for them," Nay Nay added.

"The bad news is, everybody, and I mean everybody, had a different name for them bitches. Nobody knew their real names."

"Aiight look," Eeyore said, "we need to find these bitches. We know what they look like and we know what their hustle is. IG and Facebook confirmed that much."

"So what'chu sayin' big fella?" Honcho asked, anxious.

"The whole ODH is going out to the clubs this weekend. We split up, take pictures of the bitches with us, and see what we come up with. Something gotta shake."

Every male and female from the projects that helped them out, Eeyore, Honcho, and Hondo bought them an outfit and a pair of shoes of their choice. They also gave each person two hundred dollars in spending money. They hoped the net they were casting over the city this weekend paid off.

They chose seven clubs to cover. Kim and KoKo would go to The Paparrazi. K said he'd go to Selects. Nay Nay and Bird would go to Lux. Honcho chose BWX, for obvious reasons. Eeyore would go to S&S Lounge. Jamaican J volunteered to go to Euphoria. And Hondo was left with Loafers.

It took everybody, except Honcho, five minutes after walking into their respective clubs to realize that something else was going on in Baltimore City. The Clubs were almost empty.

They regrouped downtown at the Inner Harbor. Kim made one phone call and found out where everybody was. The Fifth Regiment Armory on Division Street was hosting a concert featuring the Toe Taggin' Posse Music Group, the Migos, Famous Dex, ASAP Ferg and Desiigner.

Hondo hit his brother to let him know where they were headed, but he didn't answer, so he texted him.

***

BWX...

Honcho sat in his truck with the hawk eye on the entrance. He was cool with his brother and the rest of the crew going to the show, he was on something else.

He spotted who he was looking for and sat up. Honcho smiled.

At three am, his target walked out the club and made his way to the parking lot. The FNS 9mm was cocked with one in the head as he got out and crept up on him.

As soon as he put his hands on the driver's side door of his Altima, he felt the cold steel against the back of his head.

"Please don't kill me."

Honcho backed up. "Turn the fuck around."

He turned around. "Aww shit," he cried out, when he saw Honcho's face, "I knew that shit was gonna come back on me."

"Fuck is you talkin' about?"

"Me lying to ya'll that night," the cocky bouncer said. "I was paid by a female to say your homeboy left with a brown-skin guy."

"That's what brought me back to you. That shit just ain't make sense to me nigga. Now, who paid you?"

"I never asked her name, I just know she was pretty as fuck."

"And what she say?"

"She just came to me and pointed you and that big dude out, and said that soon ya'll would be looking for a friend. I was told to say that he left with a brown-skin guy. That's it, I swear."

"How much she paid you?"

"A thousand dollars."

"Ah stack for that?" Honcho questioned.

"She said it was also ah incentive to keep my mouth closed."

"Guess it wasn't enough, huh dumb dumb?"

"I ain't tryna die man," he pleaded.

"Where the fuck is my homeboy then?"

"Okay, I got curious after she came to me, so I went outside to be nosy. That's when I saw her watching two guys putting your man in the trunk of ah Honda Accord."

Honcho smack the club's security repeatedly until he was unconscious. He went in his pocket, removed his wallet, got his license out and placed his wallet back in his pocket.

***

Odonnell Heights…

Three forty am, K, Honcho, Hondo, Eeyore, Crystal, Bird, Nay Nay, and KoKo was sitting around in Eeyore's trap house looking defeated after Honcho told them about his night. The other eight had no luck at the Fifth Regiment Armory. It was too packed at the Concert.

"Fuck is we gon' do now ya'll?" K asked, clearly frustrated. "It's been two weeks now."

"I think it's time to get the police involved," Bird said, causing every eye in the house to go on her. "What, I don't see nothing else working. Shit, like K said, it's been two weeks."

"We ain't calling no police Bird," Eeyore said. "Think of something else."

She sighed.

Honcho's phone rung again, for the fifth time, since they came in the house.

"Who that bro?"

(Laughs) "Gia bro. She on my back."

Hondo laughed, remembering how scared he had the gang members.

Nay-Nay stole a glance at Crystal to see if she'd reveal her feelings. If she did care about Honcho talking about another girl, her face didn't reveal it.

Eeyore's phone rung. It was a private number, so he ended the call.

"Who's that at four in the morning big fella?"

"I'on't know K, the number blocked."

All the guys looked at each other and laughed, thinking about Shyaisa, the "happily" married woman.

His phone rung again.

"Answer the phone Eeyore."

"Mind your business Bird."

"It could be Sauce," Crystal said.

It was everyone's turn to look at Crystal, but she made the most sense.

Eeyore answered the phone. "Yo."

"Big Fella, it's Sauce."

He jumped up. "It's Sauce ya'll!"

Everyone jumped up and crowded him. He put the phone on speaker.

"Where you at Sauce?'

"I don't know. But what I need is two hunnid bands. I'll give it back to you once I'm able to get—"

"Fuck all that. Where I need to take the money?"

"Nowhere. It's gonna be picked up in the 'jects."

"When?"

"You in the 'jects?"

Honcho shook his head.

"I can be there in ah hour with the money," Eeyore said.

"Big fella, this ain't what you think," he said, knowing his homeboy like he knew his own self. "It's a misunderstanding."

They looked at each other questioningly.

"Just let me know what to do Sauce."

"Get the money and get to the projects big fella." The phone clicked off.

"What was that yo?" K said.

"Hold up," Hondo said. "Time to roll out ladies. Thanks for ya'll's assistance tonight."

The four females got up and headed for the door. Before Crystal left out she threw Honcho the extra key to her house. Honcho caught the key and watched her ass on the way out.

"Something about this shit don't feel right?"

"I'm with K," Hondo said. "Fuck he mean this ain't what you think?"

"We gotta kick out two hunnid to get'em back. Sounds like a kidnapping to me," Honcho said.

"I'm going to get the bread. I'll be right back," Eeyore said and got up.

"I'm going to get my big gun," K said.

"We already strapped." Honcho pulled out his gun, wiping blood off the nose, that he didn't know was there.

Hondo raised his .41mm. "What'chu think bro?" he asked, when K left.

"It's definitely some bullshit going on bro, but whatever it is, we gonna be ready for it."

"What's up with you and Crystal?"

"Nothing. Same thing up with me and Gia. A lot of fuckin'."

"You think you'll ever settle down bro?"

Honcho looked at his twin and smirked.

"What?"

"Nigga, you know what. You in love. I can feel it," Honcho said. "I'm happy for you bro. You and Ivyana look good together. You gotta watch them extremely pretty girls though bro."

"I feel you bro. She just feels like the one."

"I'm with you bro. But if she hurt you…"

"You ain't gotta say it. I already know."

"I mean it bro, I'm gonna kill her."

Hondo knew he wasn't playing.

Chapter 16

Two hundred thousand dollars in one hundred dollar bills was stacked up on the kitchen table, after being counted four times, as they waited for Sauce to call Eeyore's phone back. The clock read five oh four am, but no one was tired. They were ready and anxious to get their homeboy back. The rifle and four guns on the table with the money was enough proof.

6:07 am…
Eeyore's phone finally rung. He answered it immediately.
"Yeah," he said, putting it on speaker.
"What's up?"
"Who's this? Where's Sauce?"
"He's safe. You got the money?"
"Yeah, but where is Sauce. Lemme talk to him."
"If you got the money, you can have him back."
"We got the money."
"We, meaning it's more than one person in there with you. Shipview right. Four of ya'll. Strapped too, Good," the caller said.

They all looked at each other and shrugged.

"Send one person to the door with the money. He can even bring a gun. We, won't be offended by it." The line went dead.

Eeyore threw all the money in a book bag and volunteered to do it. He grabbed K's SKS off the table and headed to the door.

He didn't see nobody when he opened the door. His phone rung again.

"Walk to the parking lot."

"How'd you know it would be me?"

"Sauce said it would be," he said. "Walk to the black Charger.

Eeyore saw the doors open. Sauce got out of the car with a gunman behind him.

"Throw it over here."

Eeyore threw the bag and readied the SKS.

"This ain't what you think." the guy said, grabbed the bag and opened it. He peeled through the bands until he was satisfied and left.

Eeyore hugged his homeboy and lead him in the house.

"What the fuck Sauce Walka!" Honcho yelled. "Who we gotta kill?"

Sauce hugged all his homeboys. "I ain't gon lie yo, I thought I was gonna die when they first grabbed me...

"It took me a week to find out why they snatched me. It was my connect's people. They thought I killed the connect. That was his brother that grabbed the money."

"What?" K asked.

"I told them what happened to him. It took another week to confirm what I told them."

"Why the money?" K asked.

"It's the money I owed the connect."

"Oh."

"Man, we just glad you aiight," Hondo said.

"The crazy part is, that nigga wasn't even the man. It's a bitch with the bricks. Man, if I ever catch this bitch umma split her shit open," he fumed. "This bitch kept slapping the shit outta me when I wasn't answerin' her how she wanted me to."

"What she look like Sauce?"

"That's the thing, I don't know. I never saw her face."

"We got'chu back, that's all that matters yo," K said. "If we run into her, she's dead."

9:00 am...

They filed out the house one behind the other to go to their cars. They all needed some sleep.

"Yo, one of ya'll gonna take me to get my car from the impound later?"

"I got'chu Sauce," Hondo said.

"Honcho! Watch out!" they all heard Crystal yell.

Kak - Kak - Kak - Kak - Kak - Kak!

Boom! Boom! Boom!

Kak - Kak - Kak - Kak - Kak - Kak!

It was so many guns going off at one time that the sound resembled war time over in Iraq. The gunshots seemed endless, but after five minutes they stopped. People from the projects ran over to them to check on them. K, who wasn't with them, directed two boys to get their guns from them and stash them.

Bird and Nay Nay was on the ground, where Crystal was suffering from two gunshot wounds.

Hondo crawled over to his brother. Honcho was bleeding from multiple holes in him. Hondo was so numb from seeing his brother suffering, that he was oblivious to his own gunshot wounds.

"Bro," he said, "Open ya fuckin' eyes nigga. You ain't dying today. Get the fuck up!"

Honcho smiled a bloody smile and opened his eyes. He coughed up a glob of blood.

The sirens got closer. People from all over the projects was running over to them, destroying the crime scene. Some were even removing shell casings. They were doing everything they could to protect their injured own.

The police and ambulance pulled up at the same time.

The police immediately tried to control the crime scene, but it was too many people for the four officers. The projects was in an uproar.

Two more ambulances pulled up.

"We need to get this one to Shock Trauma asap! Over here! Main artery!"

"Another one over here! He's not breathing."

"It's a woman over here!" another paramedic screamed.

It was total pandemonium in Odonnell Heights Projects. They had to call three-quarters of Southeastern District Police Station out there to tame the crowds of people.

K watched the scene unfold from his bedroom window. He was furious, watching all his homeboys and his homegirl being carted off to the hospital, fighting for their lives. Whatever the outcome was, K knew that heads was gonna roll for this act of war. If it had to be him by hisself, heads was gonna roll.

He grabbed his cell phone and dialed a number. "Yeah, AT. I gotta tell you something."

Chapter 17

Sexy, major crimes detective, Sandra Altman was beyond mad that no one would talk to her. She was told that the whole projects was outside when the police pulled up. The compromised crime scene didn't make her mood any better.

"Can you believe no one saw a fucking thing?" Woody asked, when he walked up.

"Not at all. They all saw what happened. Just like they fucked my crime scene up. The aggressors fired at least seventy rounds over there by that F-150."

"That F-150 got a lot of holes in it too. Where are all the shell casings? I know they didn't use a revolver. The holes are too big. One gun used had to have been a .41 millimeter."

"Let's go to the hospital and let the beat cops waste their time here."

"Where are they at, Bayview?"

"Yeah."

***

Woody walked in the hospital behind her, wondering why she was so passionate about Odonnell Heights. She was a good detective, but she turned into a pitbull whenever something went down in the projects or if someone from the projects name came up in an investigation.

"Are you listening to me Woody?"

"Sorry, What did you say?"

"Wake up. We have a case to solve," she said, walking off in her gray Manolo Blahnik flats.

"Hello. I'm Detective Altman, this my partner, Detective Woody."

"You're here about the Odonnell Heights catastrophe?" a police officer asked.

"Yes," she said. "Can you give me an update?"

"Two of them died on the way here. They were unable to resuscitate the female. And Russell McGowan was DOA."

"What about Hondo and Honcho Pierce and Jerome Mackey?" she asked, kinda disappointed the twins were still living. And her facial expression wasn't lost on Woody either.

"We didn't get Honcho Pierce. He was flown to University Of Maryland's Shock Trauma. They resuscitated Hondo Pierce and he's now breathing with the help of a respirator. Jerome Mackey is still in surgery."

"So none of them are able to talk?"

The police just looked at her.

"I had to ask officer," she shot back. "Where are the bodies?"

"Morgue."

"Thank you."

They opened the doors that was labelled Morgue. It was cool inside and smelled funny, but they were used to it.

"May I help you?"

They pulled out their badges. "Detectives Altman and Woody. We're here to see the victims from the Odonnell Heights shooting."

She inspected their badges and led them to a room where the bodies were on metal tables. Both bodies were already cleaned and free from blood. All the detectives saw were the holes.

"What can you tell us?"

"Officially, nothing. The autopsies haven't been done," the ME said.

"What can you tell us unofficially?" Altman pressed on.

"The female was shot twice. Once in her left cheek and once in her chest. The bullet through her cheek hit her cheekbone and came out of her left temple. There was no exit wound for the chest shot.

"The guy. He was shot five times. Four times in his chest and once in his head.

They looked over the bodies.

"Crystal, what did you see? Why are you laying here girl?" she asked, circling the dead body.

Woody looked at the dead body in deep thought. "Didn't McGowan's name come up in that shooting on Twenty-First Street?"

"Yes, it did," she confirmed. "You think this was retaliation?"

"It could be."

Altman took some notes.

***

Tamera 'AT' Huntley stormed through the emergency room doors like a strong gust of wind, in search of her nephews. She even got her old school hitta, Delvon, out of retirement to come with her.

"Excuse me." She approached the desk. "I was told my nephews was brought here."

"What's your nephew's names?"

"Hondo and Honcho Pierce. They were shot up out Odonnell Heights."

"Let me ch—"

"Excuse me," a police officer approached. "Who are you to—"

"They are my nephews. Where are they? Are they okay? Can I see them?" Delvon put his hand on her back to calm her.

"Take it easy ma'am. I can take you to his doctor. Come on."

They ran into the doctor as soon as they got off the elevator.

"Doctor Inzine, excuse me. This is Mr. Pierce's aunt.

"Hello, I'm Doctor Inzine and you are?"

"Tamera Huntley, aunt of Hondo and Honcho Pierce."

"I don't know who Honcho is, but I operated on Hondo. He fought hard and made it through surgery. He needed a blood transfusion because he lost so much blood. He was shot three times Once in the stomach, once in his left shoulder, and one time in his neck. The neck shot was clean through the side, so it sounds worser than it really is. The stomach shot was the worst. His small intestine was damaged.

"Can I see him?"

"Yes."

She started crying the second she laid eyes on her nephew. He looked so peaceful and innocent. The constant beep of the respirator was a reminder to her that life in Baltimore was very short.

She pulled out her iPhone and snapped a picture, then sent it to her sister's cell phone with the caption: I'm sorry.

"You sure that was a good idea AT?"

She just looked at Delvon, and dialed a number on her phone.

"Yeah AT."

"Where are you?"

"We all in the lobby," K said.

"Honcho is not here."

"They say Honcho went to Shock Trauma."

"Shock Trauma!" AT screamed. She hung up the phone. She approached Hondo and placed her hand on his face lovingly. "Baby, who did this to you," she whispered. "Come back to me baby. You not done with this world yet."

"Excuse me."

AT and Delvon turned around. They were both shocked to see who was standing in the doorway. It was a ghost from their past.

"What the fuck you doing here bitch?" AT yelled. Delvon had to hold AT back.

"I'm here doing my job, Tamera."

"Bitch don't say my name like we friends. I can't stand you. You lucky Delvon right here bitch, 'cause I'd beat your ass in here."

"Are you threatening a Baltimore City Police Officer?"

Delvon's mouth dropped open. AT just smiled.

"It don't surprise me none BITCH. You were always a snake, a pig, and rat."

"My name isn't Bitch, nor is it snake, pig, or rat. It's Detective Sandra Altman," she smiled.

Chapter 18

Tammy couldn't see the photo on her phone no more. The tears prevented her from seeing anything. She was beyond angry. Mainly because she had an idea of who was responsible for her boy's shooting.

She got up off her bunk, washed her face, and stashed her phone. She took the sheet off her cell door.

Her celly saw her face and ran over to her. "TT what's up? Who we ready to fuck up?"

"I'm gon' see this bitch Kimberly."

"Hold up," Lil' China said. She ran to the cell, grabbed her knife, and came back. "Come on TT."

They saw Kimberly telling extravagant war stories about her gang and her. She must've felt TT close by. When she turned around TT and Lil' China was right there.

"How you be getting in touch with London's bitch-ass?" she asked, knowing they worshipped London. Tammy knew he wasn't a bitch, but she loved disrespecting him in front of them.

"T - T- I—"

"I ain't know you stutter Kimberly. Look, you know I be talking to the nigga, but I don't know the new number."

"I'll get it to you."

"I need it now. This important," she said, trying her best to remain calm.

"Alright," she said and walked away.

"You got a problem with your eyes Missy?"

"Lil' China ain't nobody paying you no attention."

"Good bitch."

Missy sighed and then smiled.

"Her you go TT," Kimberly said. "I need to holla at you later too."

"Aiight," Tammy said and walked away. On the way back to their cell, she told her about what happened to her sons and her theory.

"You wanna get these bitches? I hate them bitches anyway," Lil' China said.

"Let me holla at this nigga London first. Hold me down." She walked in the cell and put the sheet up.

London answered on the second ring.

"Yeah."

"What's up?"

"Who this?"

"TT muthafucka."

"Oh, hey. I know what'chu callin' about, that shit been all over the news TT."

"And."

"I asked around TT, it wasn't the gang. They say it wasn't them. They were all told to leave them alone."

"Yeah, I heard about the red light you put on my boys. Thanks and no thanks. That shit ain't save them. You got a few renegades that's running shit on their own. Not caring about the red light," she said, through clenched teeth. "I want them muthafuckers who did this to my boys. If I don't get them, we'll assume it was the last people they was beefing with and go at them."

"Come on TT, why the threats? You know umma do all I can to find out what happened to my god-sons. They are my family too. Don't do shit until I call you. Aiight?"

"Aiight. Twenty-four hours," she said and hung up.

***

Johns Hopkins Bayview…

Fifty plus people, kids included, loitered the emergency room waiting room, looking for answers.

AT finally made it to them. They all stopped talking when she appeared.

"I appreciate you all for coming, showing your support for our fallen. Hondo is upstairs fighting for his life. Sauce is out of surgery and recovering." She paused to compose herself. "Honcho was flown to University's Shock Trauma where he's already had three surgeries. He's fighting, just like his brother." Tears crawled down her face. "I'm sorry ya'll. Crystal and Eeyore didn't make it."

People started screaming and crying, causing the kids to scream and cry. Shyasia fell out. K left, he had to get some type of relief. Bird, Nay Nay, and Ko Ko cried and consoled one another. The blow was devastating to all tenants of the ODH Projects. Eeyore was loved by all, and Crystal, she was a little standoffish, but she was family and her cooking on the grill was second to none.

London Junior walked in the hospital with three of his goons. Those in the know looked at him with disdain. He ignored the looks and went straight to AT.

"You okay AT?'

"What kind of question is that? Fuck no I'm not okay."

"You know what I mean."

"I don't know shit. You wanna make me feel better? Get out there and find out who did this to them. Put some money out there. I'll put it up if you don't have it. Tomorrow's Sunday, I want the ma'fuckas who did this by Wednesday."

"Okay AT," London Junior said, shaking his head.

Detective Sandra Altman and her partner stood off to the side taking notes and mental pictures of everyone in the waiting room. There would be retaliation and when it happened, she'd be there.

***

MCIJ...

London had been pacing his cell ever since he got off the phone with TT. He didn't know what to do. He lied to TT and he knew it'd come back to bite him in his ass. Once they found out that the gang was responsible, nothing would stop them from getting revenge.

His phone vibrated in his pocket snapping him out of stressing. "Hello."

"It's me pops."

"You find them two stupid ma'fuckas?'

"Yeah, I found them."

"And what they say?"

"They said they ain't do it, but I know they did. They were acting guilty. After I made it seem like it was nothing, they confessed."

"Shit!"

"This is bad pops."

"Who you tellin'," he said. "Who else they told?"

"They said they told Gooz."

"Oh, they good as dead. Super stupid ma'fuckers!"

"AT gave me four days to come up with some names."

"Shit, TT gave me twenty-four hours."

"And Delvon was up the hospital with her."

"Damn, she called Delvon. It's 'bout to get real ugly son, If it haven't' already."

"What'chu want me to do pops?"

"Honestly son, I want you to disappear. It's about to get ugly for our people. You'll be included in that once they feel like you with the gang and sooner or later you'll have to show where your loyalty at."

"What about AT and TT?"

"Fuck'em. But make no mistake about it, them bitches are dangerous. Be careful London," he warned his soon.

"I'm good pops. I ain't going no where either.

"London, I only told you stories about AT and TT. Artillery Tamera and Taliban Tammy. They are two treacherous bitches. Watch AT," he said, rubbing his arm unconsciously.

"Pop," he laughed, "AT is like my mother. She ain't gon' do shit to me; her old ass. And if she do try some shit, my guns ain't prejudice."

London shook his head at his son's arrogance. He knew that most kids in Baltimore City, that was in the streets, carried that same arrogance. Which is why they were dying at an alarming rate.

"Just be careful son," was all he said.

"Aiight pops."

Chapter 19

After they stopped the main artery bleeding in Honcho's side, and had the emergency blood transfusion surgery he went to Hopkins Bayview with his brother. Sauce was released from the hospital a week later. He was shot in his arm and left hand only. Hondo was breathing on his own and was slowly getting back to himself.

AT was trying her best to keep the police away from her nephews, but it was only so much that she could do. She had her lawyer on standby for when Altman and Woody came back.

Sauce handled all of the arrangements for Crystal and Eeyore's funeral. Some of the two hundred thousand dollars that he owed Eeyore was spent on the double funeral. Crystal didn't have any family to come through, so the whole projects stepped up. Sauce even had a video director record the whole funeral for the twins.

In two weeks time, the streets knew who was behind the Odonnell Heights shooting. The gang claimed responsibility after Gooz said he had it done for his mother. The two true trigger men was only known by the twins because they saw them and was the closest to the shooters. Honcho also knew one of the gunmen from doing time with him.

Honcho, who shared a hospital room with his twin brother, explained to him who the one shooter was. Neither brother told a soul, not even Sauce. But since Sauce knew it was the gang who did it, him, K, and Jamaican J was hitting all the gang's hotspots. The heavy presence of police out ODH Projects prevented the gang from retaliating.

***

Johns Hopkins Bayview…

Hondo had his phone up to his face blushing and smiling as he face timed with Ivyana. She had been there for him as much as he allowed her to be. She wasn't happy with not being able to come to Baltimore to be with him, but she respected his wishes and stayed in DC.

"You're terrible you know that?"

"How?" Hondo smiled.

"I should be there with you babe, and you know it."

"Not this again."

"Yes, this again."

Detectives Altman and Woody walked in his room.

"Aww shit."

"What babe," Ivyana asked.

"The pigs are here."

"Pigs?"

"Cops. Police. Swine."

"Oh, what you want me to call you back?"

Altman tried to see who was on the screen, but he held the phone to his chest.

"Excuse you. Nosy ass cop!"

"Who is that?" she asked.

Woody looked at his partner in shock.

Hondo ended the call and cleared his call log. "What's up with your partner yo?"

Wood shrugged his shoulders.

"Who was on the phone Mr. Pierce?"

"Why the fuck you care?"

"Give me your phone."

"You got a warrant?"

She huffed in frustration. Woody stepped up.

"Mr. Pierce, we're here to talk about the shooting in your neighborhood."

"Who was on—"

"Enough with the phone already detective," Woody said, fed up. "Do you need a moment?"

"No," she said, getting herself together.

"Okay."

"I don't know who shot me. I don't remember much from that day."

"You don't remember firing a weapon Mr. Pierce?"

"Don't answer shit Hondo," AT said, pushing Honcho's hospital bed into the room. "Bitch, didn't I tell you to stay away from my nephews?"

"Tamera, for the tenth time, I'm doing my job and my name ain't bitch."

"Excuse me sir, what's your name?"

"Detective Woody ma'am."

"Woody, listen, I don't like this bitch. I never liked this bitch. So if you looking for cooperation, you ain't gon' get it with her."

Woody nodded once. "Let's go detective."

"No, we haven't—"

"Now!"

She looked down at Hondo's phone one last time and left out.

"That bitch crazy," Honcho said.

"Where you know her from AT?"

AT sighed. "She is me and your mother's arch enemy."

"She knows Momma too?"

"Yes, She grew up in Odonnell Heights too," she said, dropping the jaws of her nephews. "She use to mess with your father."

"What!?"

"Pops was fuckin' her?"

"Yes. He was. Until he met my sister. Your mother took your father from her. She tried to fight Tammy. Tammy beat her ass, then after she beat her ass, we jumped her. She hated us because she felt like Tammy stole her life. Your father was getting money too. At first, your mother took him from her just because we ain't like her, but your father fell in love and eventually so did your mother.

"At that time London had been tryna get me. I was curving his ass at first, but then I gave in. Sandra couldn't get Clyde from your mother, so she set her eyes on London. She got'em too. She couldn't wait to tell me. Ah bitch," she said with disgust. "But London was more of ah bitch for cheating on me, so me and your mother beat him with bats. We broke his motherfuckin' arm and leg."

The twins laughed.

"I stopped fucking with him. He started fucking with her. Got her pregnant with his child. I think the bitch was lying. She wanted to be Tammy so bad."

"You ain't know she was a police?"

"Fuck no."

"AT, that lady been harassing me for years," Hondo said.

"So listen. London came to my house one night crying, talking about she killed his baby. I'm not gonna lie, I still loved London, so I let his sorry ass in that night. Me and your mother think she was lying about being pregnant. She moved out the projects after that.

"I didn't take London's sorry ass back. That was in ninety-two, the year ya'll was born. London Junior came in ninety-four. His mother wasn't shit. Another money hungry bitch. I had London Junior more than she did. Then one day she just up and disappeared. London never said shit about it, so neither did I. Tammy thinks he killed her for stealing from him. I don't know. I know I raised her son."

"This some urban novel shit. AT, you might can sell your story to that nigga Kayo from the city."

"This is some urban novel shit, Honcho." She walked over to him and fixed his covers. "You okay baby?"

"Yeah AT. I'm good."

"You need your bag changed Hondo?"

Everytime he thought about the colostomy bag or someone mentioned it, he got mad. He hated his defect and only blood would make him feel better.

"It's okay baby. You won't have it long."

"Don't trip bro. We gon' get up out this shit. And when we do..."

"You already."

Chapter 20

Woody sat in the passenger seat of their car staring at her, waiting for her to explain her actions, But she didn't, she just kept looking out the window.

"So you just not gonna say shit?"

"What?"

"Your actions back there. I need you to explain them. I don't wanna fuck this case up, so I also need you to explain your relationship with this family."

She kept quiet.

"Well then, you leave me with no choice but to report your actions to the shift commander."

She let ten minutes pass before she said, "I grew up in Odonnell Heights. The guy that was killed, Russell McGowan, his mother was a friend of mine. The twins' aunt; Tamera Huntley and her twin sister Tammy Huntley was friends, but we had a falling out. Anything else?"

"It's deeper than that. I'm no idiot."

"Okay, I despise the twins. They are dangerous, they are criminals, and I know it was passed on to the Pierce twins."

"Was that Tammy we ran into first?"

"Oh no. Tammy is doing thirty-six years for murder two. Although identical, she's the worst of the two."

"And you think you should be working this case? You're too close to this Altman. You can barely contain yourself around them. And look how you reacted about Hondo's phone. What was that about?"

Woody asked, trying to get a clear understanding.

"I thought that… never mind. I'm fine. I can work the case. I will do better."

"I don't think you will."

"Come on Woody. You know I'm a great detective."

"Never said you wasn't. I think this is to close for you."

"Trust me. I'm fine."

Woody thought about. "Okay. I won't say anything, but I'm taking the point on this. And if I say "fall back" you do so, no questions asked."

As bad as she didn't want to give up the lead detective (point) spot on the case, she had to, so she did.

"Okay. Your lead. I'll follow you," she said.

***

Johns Hopkins Bayview…

Tamera was on the phone with her sister, while the twins gave the doctor and nurses a hard time for nothing more than out of boredom.

"Honcho, you're going to bust your wounds open if you continue moving around."

"Doc, I'm getting bedsores. I gotta get up."

"You'll be okay Honcho."

"Aye doc, when can I get this shit bag off?"

"Hondo, it'll be weeks, maybe months, before that comes off."

"This some bullshit yo!"

"That's Hondo, fussing about his colostomy bag," AT said, into her phone. "Your mother said chill boy."

"This some bullshit," he mumbled.

London Junior appeared in the door once the doctor left.

"What's up family?"

They all looked at the doorway.

"You must got some good news we can use nigga. That's why you're here?"

"Damn AT, no how you doing, no nothing?"

"Do you have any bullet holes in you London?" How about a collapsed lung? Or how about a shit bag?" He shook his head. "I didn't think so. I already know how you doing nigga."

"Damn AT, you cold."

"When it comes to my nephews, I don't give a fuck."

"AT, you helped raised me. I'm practically your son," he said, genuinely hurt that Tamera was treating him like an outsider.

Tamera jumped up out her chair so quick, it scared him a little. Close enough to kiss him she said, "So practically, that would make you their cousin. First cousin. If Hondo was laying in that bed alone and Honcho was out there, bodies would be dropping. He wouldn't be out there partying nigga," she said, and showed the photos of him on IG last night at the club with his gang member friends. A few of them even showed him holding the gang's beloved gray bandanna.

"Cat got'chu tongue bro?" Honcho asked.

"If I knew who did it—"

"Stop," Hondo said, holding up his hand "Don't do that London. You ain't gotta do that. All I say is that when we come, don't be in the way."

He sighed. They saw right through his lies. They knew just like he knew who was responsible. London Junior left the hospital unsure of where he stood with the only family he'd ever known.

"We gon' kill his ass too for playin' bent. Bitch-ass nigga," Honcho said.

"I changed his fucking diapers, so you know he don't value family. He's gone off that gang shit. I guess we gon' have to show him how the fuck we get down."

"Yeah AT."

"Yeah AT shit. When are you gonna let that pretty girl come up here and be with you?"

"Damn AT, you all up in my personal business."

"Hondo, don't make me smack yo' ass. You are my personal business and that girl loves you."

"You don't even know her AT."

"I met her the other day." Tamera smiled.

"Oh gawd," he said and put his head under the covers.

Honcho laughed at his brother to play off his thoughts. His mind was really focused on killing London Junior. Eeyore had warned them about him for years. *He had to go,* he thought.

Chapter 21

(October 2017)

Three months flew by and things had calmed down in the streets. Sauce and K had killed a good amount of gang members and the twins was out of the hospital.

Hondo finally allowed Ivyana to take care of him. She made the trip everyday from DC to Baltimore without fuss. He used their time together to really get to know her. And the more he learned, the deeper he fell in love. They shared a lot in common they found out. He mistakenly thought she was a spoiled brat that came from money. She was a hustler like him. The white Porsche Macan GTS that she drove and the eight thousand-dollar all white Saint Laurent gown that she wore on the night they met at BWX should've been a dead giveaway. Ivyana was everything he ever wanted in one woman.

For Ivyana, she wasn't' trying to fall in love, but his boldness in the club on the night they met rocked her world. She still giggled at the thought of him smelling her feet and breath in the club. To add to that his tight knit family was something that she yearned. It had been her and her sister by themselves, holding each other down, no parents, just them. AT and Honcho took her in as family. She even talked to TT on the phone.

***

Ivyana laid in the bed with the covers halfway covering her naked body, thinking of the pleasurable hurting that Hondo put on her last night.

She finally got up, wrapped up in the sheets and went to find her man. She found him in the basement working out. She watched him for a minute, before making herself known. He didn't hear her come down the steps, because Kevin Gates was playing too loud.

"What's up baby?" he asked, looking up.

"I didn't know where you was. You want breakfast?" He pointed to her. "You ate enough of me last night. I mean real food. Eggs, turkey bacon, grits, french toast."

"All that sounds good. Yeah babe, make it. Make enough for three, Honcho on his way over."

"Okay baby."

An hour later. Ivyana was clearing the dining room table so she could wash the dishes.

"You gotta marry her bro. She cook and clean," Honcho said and laughed, holding his side.

"You still hurting?'

"Just a little.

"The lies you tell. I can tell you still hurting."

"I'm good bro. Listen, that information came back. I know where dude at."

Hondo's eyes lit up immediately.

"That's why I came over here. I fuckin' found his bitch-ass." Honcho was extremely excited.

"What's the plan?" Hondo asked.

"This nigga is careful, I had someone watching him. The only way we are gonna get him is by…"

***

Guilford Avenue…

Hondo was parked in the black van on 21st Street, while Honcho was parked on 22nd Street in a dark blue van. Both of them were dressed in all black, with gloves on and a ski mask rolled up on their head. Sauce was boldly parked on Guilford Avenue, directly in front of the Parole & Probation building. Jamaican J was waiting on his signal, while K was sitting on someone's steps across the street.

They were all strapped and waiting for Twon to come out of the building. The twins was itching to get Twon. They couldn't stop thinking about him and Maniac. It only took ten thousand to get one of the gang memes to flip and tell everything. Honcho didn't think Big Day Day would flip at first, but money talked and he spilled his guts. He wanted to set all his homies up after getting paid. He was offering Honcho all types of information.

K jumped up and swiftly made his way across the street. That was the signal. Jamaican J pulled his ski mask down and got ready. Hondo and Honcho did the same.

Sauce watched K bump Twon. An argument quickly ensued.

"Aye bro, fuck that nigga. Smack his ass and come on," someone yelled for an Infiniti G37.

The three occupants of the G37 was so focused on Twon and K, that they never saw Sauce walk up to the car with the SKS. Twon saw him though.

Kak! Kak! Kak! Kak! Kak! Sauce worked the weapon with skill in broad day light.

Twon tried to run back in Parole & Probation but K tripped him. K ran inside and held the doors. Twon got up and ran towards 21st Street.

When he tried to cross the street, he was blindsided by a car. Jamaican J gave Hondo the thumbs up and pulled off. Hondo pulled up on him and put him in the van and pulled off. Two blocks over he switched cars, taped Twon up with duct tape, put him in the trunk, set the van on fire and pulled off smooth, free, and clear.

***

One of the most brazen acts of violence happened today on this East Baltimore Street behind me; right in front of Parole & Probation on Guilford Avenue. Authorities believe one gunman opened fire on a car in front of the building. The car held three self proclaimed gang members. All three men died on the scene and one more who is believed to have been the target is still missing after running from the scene.

One witness claim she saw the man run from the scene, only to be hit by a car shortly after. While laying on the ground, she claims, a black van pulled up and a suspect wearing a black ski mask got out and put the man inside the van.

Polices are confirming that they found a black van two streets over engulfed in flames. Residents are encouraged to call the police if you have any information regarding what happened here today. Back to you Gail.

Chapter 22

Hondo looked at the TV and smiled.

"You happy now babe?" Ivyana asked.

"Not yet I'm not." Hondo held his woman tight. "What do you want Ivyana?"

"I want you baby."

"Forever?"

"Forever and a day," she said, confidently.

"You got my back?"

"Like I'm the tag on your shirt."

(Laughs) "That's what I'm talking about."

"I'm not just a pretty face Hondo. I'm not a bill either."

"What are you then?" he asked.

"An asset."

Hondo smiled, feeling like he hit the lottery.

***

Later that night, Hondo met up with Honcho and they went to where they had Twon still in the trunk of the car.

They pulled him out the trunk and dragged him to the middle of the abandoned field. Hondo removed the duck tape from his mouth.

"What's up Twon?"

"What's up?"

"Oh, you gon' play tough?" Honcho asked.

"Tough? Nawww. Not at all," Twon said. "I know what it is. I knew what it was when I was seven years old."

They just looked at each other.

"Where is Maniac?"

(Laughs) "Ya'll jokin' right?"

They cocked the FN Five Sevens that they carried.

"You sure you don't wanna tell us where Maniac at?"

"Now why would I wanna do some shit like that?"

"We gonna find'em, just like we found you," Hondo said.

"Go ahead and kill me and do it quick. I'm ready," he said, closing his eyes. They raised their guns. "Only thing I regret is not killin' you niggas. I let my father down."

"Ya father can mourn you nigga."

"My father dead. You should know, one of ya'll killed him.

"If ya homeboy ain't come around our 'hood playin', we would've never went up Barclay Street."

(Laughs) "That was my sister ya'll killed, not my father. He was killed in nineteen ninety-nine."

(Laughs) "Ninety-nine? Nigga, we was seven!"

"Yeah, I know. So was I. One of ya'll killed my father."

The twins looked at each other knowingly.

"Yeah, ya'll know the story," he said, opening his eyes. "My father, my uncle and London rushed ya'll house back in the day to rob ya'll house. Ya father bucked and whipped out on my uncle. London shot your father twice in the head. Your mother came out firing wild shots, until she saw ya father dead. She dropped the gun and ran over to your father. My father went to put two in ya mother's head and one of ya'll come out of no where and shot my father three times in his chest. London dragged my uncle out of there before he could kill ya'll."

Both twins stood shocked at Twon's admission. There was no doubt that they believed him. The only people that knew about Hondo killing the intruder was them, their mother and the two remaining masked intruders. They never even told their aunt AT.

"Ya'lls faces is priceless," he laughed.

Bok! Bok! Bok! Bok!

Bok! Bok! Bok! Bok!

Twon's body hit the dirt with a deathly thud. Honcho went in his pocket and took everything out.

"This fuckin' bitch-ass nigga London bro."

Honcho hugged his brother. "We gon' get'em all bro. All of them dying."

Chapter 23

October 23rd…

At twelve noon the doors opened to the Division Of Corrections and out walked a bad ass forty-five years young woman. Long black hair, light brown eyes, 5'8" and full of hate.

AT was leaned up against her Audi. She held her arms out for her twin sister. Tammy "TT" Huntley hugged her sister and held on for dear life.

"Don't you ever leave me again Tammy. I did everyday of that eighteen years with you."

"I know you did AT. I'm not going nowhere. I love you sis'."

"I love you more."

They got in the car. AT handed her sister ten thousand dollars in pocket money and a palm size .380 ACP semi-auto.

"Take me Down Da Hill real quick AT," she said and began changing in the clothes that At bought her.

"Pull over right here. What time is it sis?"

"Twelve seventeen pm sis. Why?"

"This store right here. It's special to me."

"How so?"

"A friend of mine work here."

"You was never a good liar."

A woman came out the store with a nurse outfit on. She walked down the side street. TT got out.

"Brenda. Aye Brenda. Wait up"

The lady stopped. "Do I know you?"

"No. But I'm a close friend of your sister. You are the one that be holding Kimberly down right?'

"Yeah, you got something for her?"

"Sure do." TT pulled out the gun. **Boom! Boom!** "Tell'em TT sent'chu bitch."

She jumped in the car and AT pulled off.

"Welcome home sis'."

"Thanks. It's good to be home. Now take me to my boys."

Epilogue

Sister's Haven Bar & Lounge…

Tammy 'TT' Huntley was surrounded by her love ones and some unofficial extended family from Odonell Heights Projects. TT didn't care, she had her sister and her two boys back in her life and that's all that mattered.

"Momma, I'm happy you home."

"Yeah Momma," Hondo agreed.

"I'm happy to be home," she said, kissing each boy's cheek.

"Smile," Tamera said, with her camera. She snapped a few pictures, then let K snap a few pictures of all of them.

"Hondo, where's that pretty girlfriend of yours?'

"She on her way Momma. She wanted to pick you up a gift."

"When are you gonna get a girlfriend bad-ass boy?"

"As soon as I meet Ivyana's sister," he shot back.

"So what are ya'll doing?"

"We got the crack out the way."

"Yeah, they bought some coke from me TT."

"I need to get me some money. I got some things I wanna do," Tammy said.

"Momma, we need to talk about some serious shit. Not tonight though."

"Yeah Momma," Honcho said, "After we handle this business you can get the dope business out the way"

"What about Sauce?" she asked.

"He don't want nothing to do with the drug game after he got snatch."

"Oh okay."

"Yeah, he ready to open a fitness center."

"There go Ivyana right there Momma."

They all looked at the entrance. She dropped jaws when she came in.

"I'm gonna have some pretty grandbabies.

They all laughed.

Hondo stood up and kissed his girl. "You already know AT and you've spoken to my mother before, but here she go in person. Momma, this is Ivyana. Ivyana, this is my mother Tammy aka TT."

They hugged one another. "Take care of my baby," she whispered in her ear.

"I will. What shall I call you?"

"Momma or TT."

Sauce walked over to them and handed Tammy a bottle of Ace or Spade. "Welcome home TT."

"Thanks Sauce baby," she said, kissing his cheek.

"Baby I got a surprise for you," Ivyana said.

Sauce looked at Ivyana. The look in his eyes was pure hatred.

"What" I got something on my face," she asked him.

"Bitch! Umma kill you!" he yelled and wrapped his massive hands around her little neck. "Bitch!"

"Sauce!" Hondo yelled and jumped up. Honcho was right behind him.

Everyone was trying to stop Sauce from choking the life out of Ivyana.

"Let go Sauce!" Honcho yelled. "Fuck is you doing nigga?!"

"Jerome Mackey, if you don't take your fuckin' hands from around that girl's neck umm—"

"She the one that kidnapped me Momma TT," he yelled, releasing her.

Tha Twinz 2
'Family Secrets'
Coming Soon

Excerpt

**An Abandon Warehouse
In Southeast DC…**

Sauce didn't know what to think while he sat, strapped, in the chair inside of a dark, dank, cold building. He didn't know where he was or how long he had been unconscious. He did know someone hit him in his head with a gun when he was on his way to his car.

"What the fuck," he said. "Bitch-ass gang niggas."

Two big guys walked in his line of sight. They didn't have masks on, which was a bad sign to him. They stood in front of him with their arms folded across their chest.

"That shit don't scare me my niggas."

"It ain't us you gotta be scared of," the taller one said.

Sauce was positive he had never seen either one of them before.

"What the fuck ya'll want?" Sauce asked.

"It ain't what we want," the shorter one said. "It's what "she" want."

The taller one put a black, cloth bag over his head. Two minutes later he heard some heels clicking on the floor.

"He say anything?"

"Nothing important."

"Take the bag off his head and just cover his eyes. I need access to his face."

He still didn't see her when they removed the bag, but she was close. He could smell her. His eyes was covered with some kind of cloth that he couldn't see through.

"Okay," she said, walking in front of him, "This is how this is gonna work. I ask the questions. You answer them. If I ask what color you got on, you say white. Not white and why you got on white. You understand me so far?"

"Yeah."

"What's ya name?"

"What?"

The smack was swift, hard, and unexpected.

"I thought you said you understood me?" she asked. "Let's try this again. I ask the questions, you answer me. If I ask you what color do you have on, you answer… what?"

"White."

"I can't hear you."

"White," he said, through clenched teeth.

"We gonna get along real good." She paced the floor, then asked, "What's your name?"

"Sauce."

"Good. You're a natural," she said. "Sauce, did you kill Malik to keep my money?"

"What?"

She punched him in his jaw, ringing his ears.

"Fuck! Just tell me what the fuck you want?"

She threw two more punches. Those got him woozy a bit.

"You fucking up Sauce. I told you how this work," she said and smacked him real hard. "Now, did you kill Malik to keep my money?"

"No."

"Did you kill Malik?"

"No."

"Who killed him then, if it wasn't you?"

"A gang member name Mularu."

"And where does this Mularu be?"

"Twenty-first and Barclay Street."

"Where is my money?"

"I don't know what money you talking about."

She was contemplating was that an answer or not.

"You did business with Malik?"

"Yes."

"So then you were doing business with me, because he worked for me. Understand that. What was Mularu's beef with Malik?"

"They didn't have beef. I don't even think they knew each other."

"So why did he kill him?"

"I'm beefin' with his gang."

"So he got killed because of you?"

"Yes," Sauce said. "Can I say something?"

"Go ahead."

"Mularu is dead. I killed him along with a few more of his gang member friends. I fucked with Malik. He was always good to me."

After he spoke, they left. It felt like an eternity before someone came and fed him a cheeseburger and water. Then it was silence again.

"Okay, your story checks out," she said days later when they came back. "You wanna go home? Where's my money? My two hundred thousand dollars?"

He was broken at that point. His once white Versace outfit was soiled with urine and feces. He was beyond mad and wanted to break the woman's neck that put her hands on him. He promised his self he'd find her. But for now, he figured he'd submit.

"I got the money."

"Where, I want it?"

"I'll make the call."

The guy handed her the phone. "Gimmie the number."

She blocked her number and called the number Sauce gave her. It went to voice mail immediately.

"Your boys ain't fucking with you."

"Call back," he said.

She did.

"Yo," he answered.

"Big fella, it's Sauce."

OTHER

BOOKS

BY KAYO

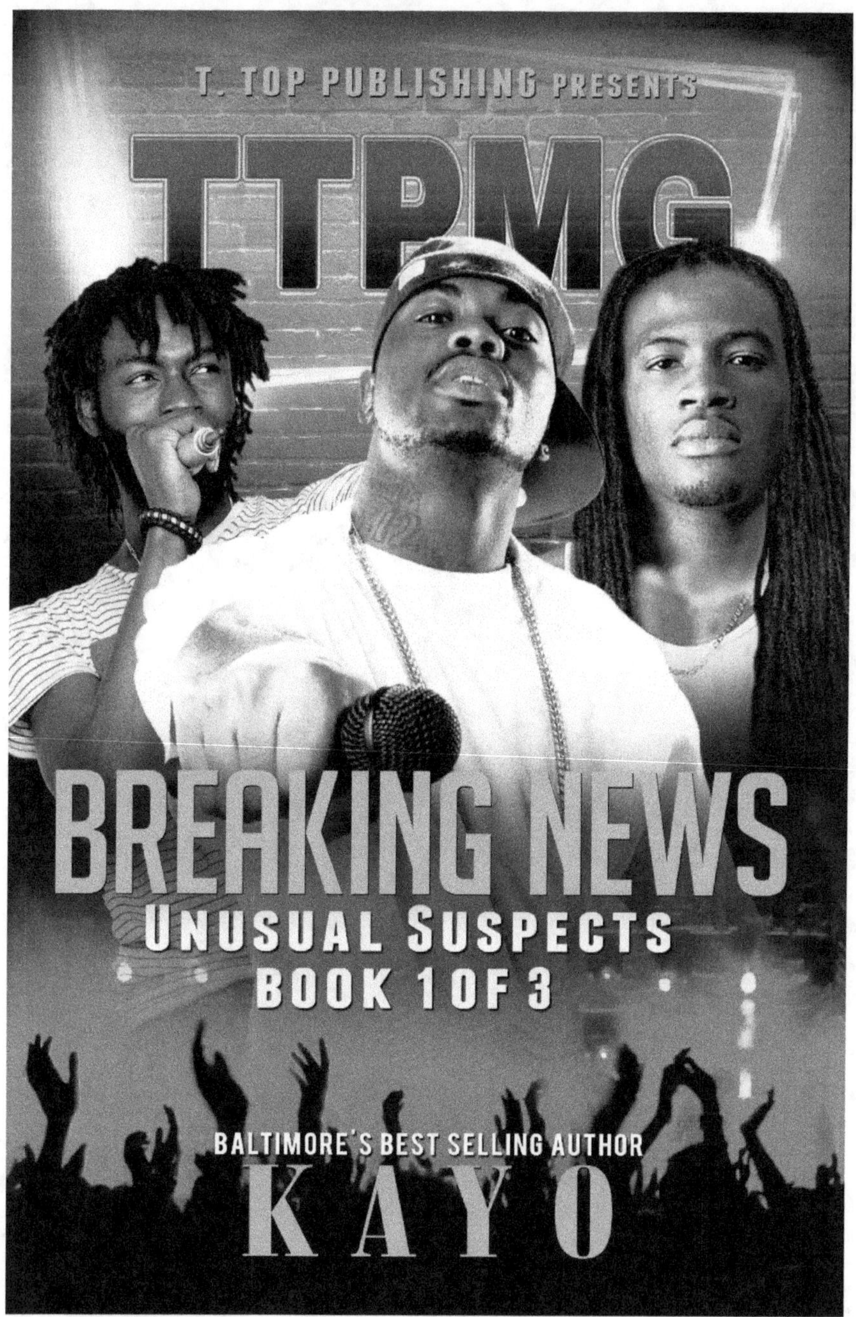
T. TOP PUBLISHING PRESENTS
TTPMG
BREAKING NEWS
UNUSUAL SUSPECTS
BOOK 1 OF 3
BALTIMORE'S BEST SELLING AUTHOR
KAYO

T. TOP PUBLISHING PRESENTS
BREAKING NEWS
BOOK 2 OF 3
BALTIMORE'S BEST SELLING AUTHOR
KAYO

T. TOP PUBLISHING PRESENTS
FRIENEMIES
Who Kan You Trust
BOOK 1 OF 10
BALTIMORE'S BEST SELLING AUTHOR
KAYO

T. TOP PUBLISHING presents
FRIENEMIES
Shhh Stop Snitchin' 2
BOOK 2 OF 10
BALTIMORE'S BEST SELLING AUTHOR
KAYO

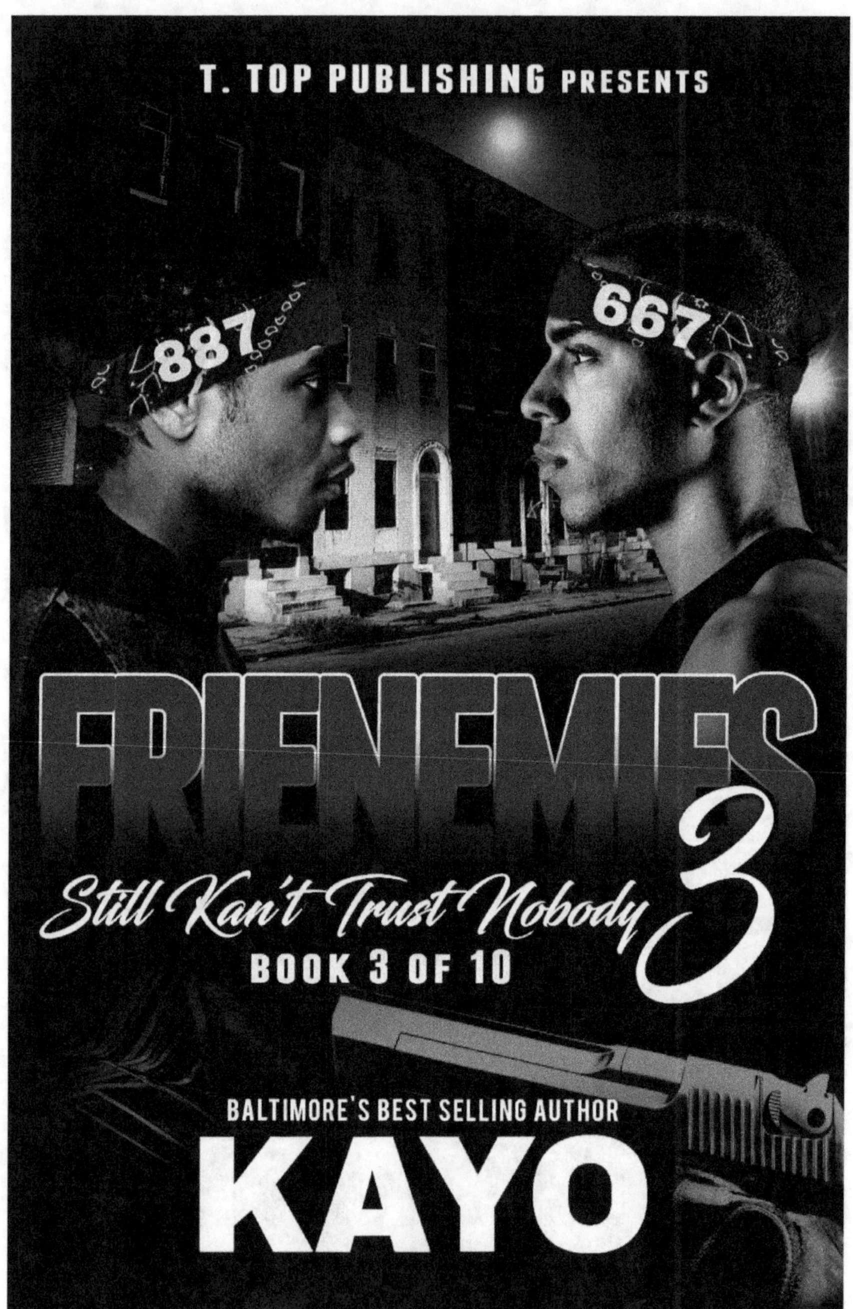
T. TOP PUBLISHING PRESENTS
887
667
FRIENEMIES
Still Kan't Trust Nobody 3
BOOK 3 OF 10
BALTIMORE'S BEST SELLING AUTHOR
KAYO

T. TOP PUBLISHING PRESENTS
4 HUNNID
FRIENEMIES
4 Ever Tree Top
BOOK 4 OF 10
4
BALTIMORE'S BEST SELLING AUTHOR
KAYO

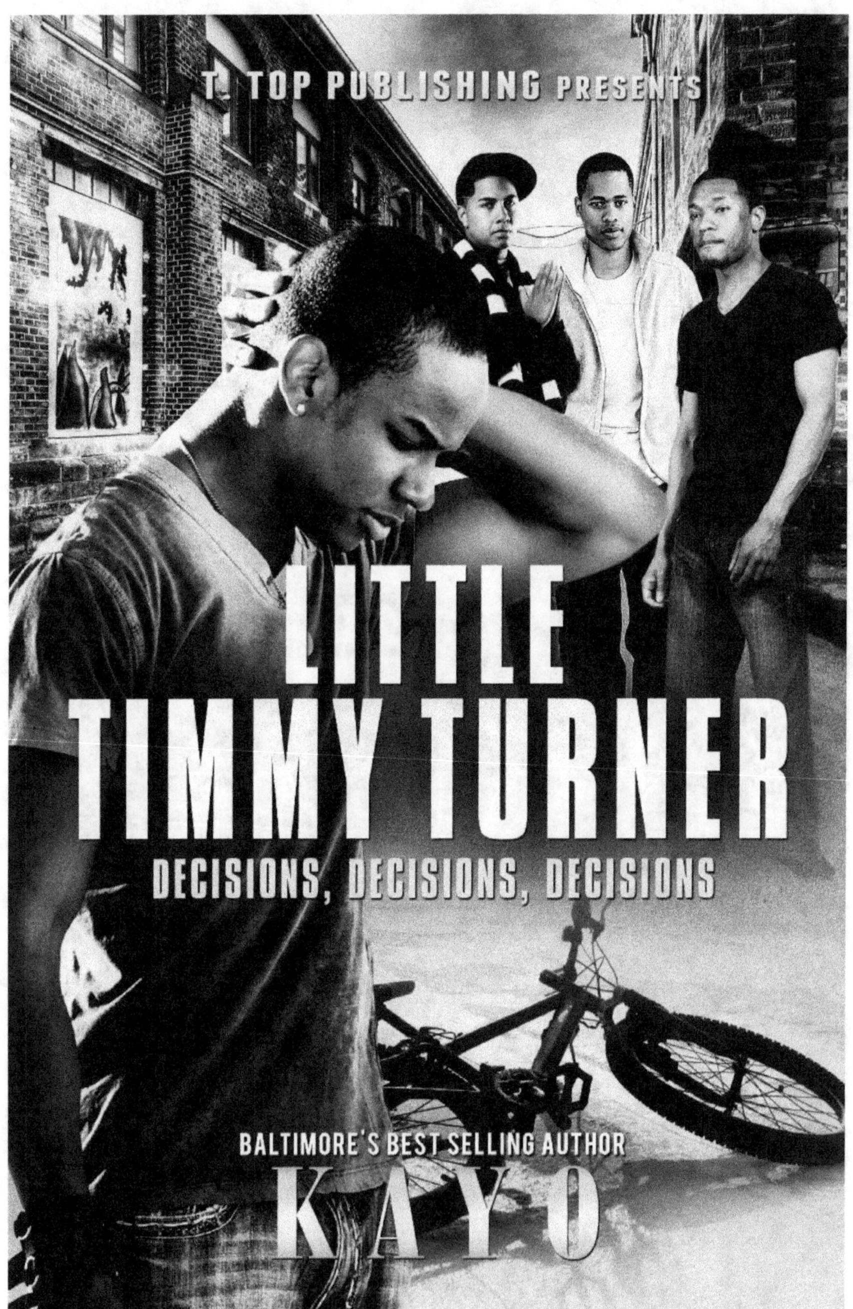
T. TOP PUBLISHING PRESENTS
LITTLE
TIMMY TURNER
DECISIONS, DECISIONS, DECISIONS
BALTIMORE'S BEST SELLING AUTHOR
KAYO

T. TOP PUBLISHING PRESENTS
She's My ROCK
MEECHIE & KYRA
BALTIMORE'S BEST SELLING AUTHOR
KAYO

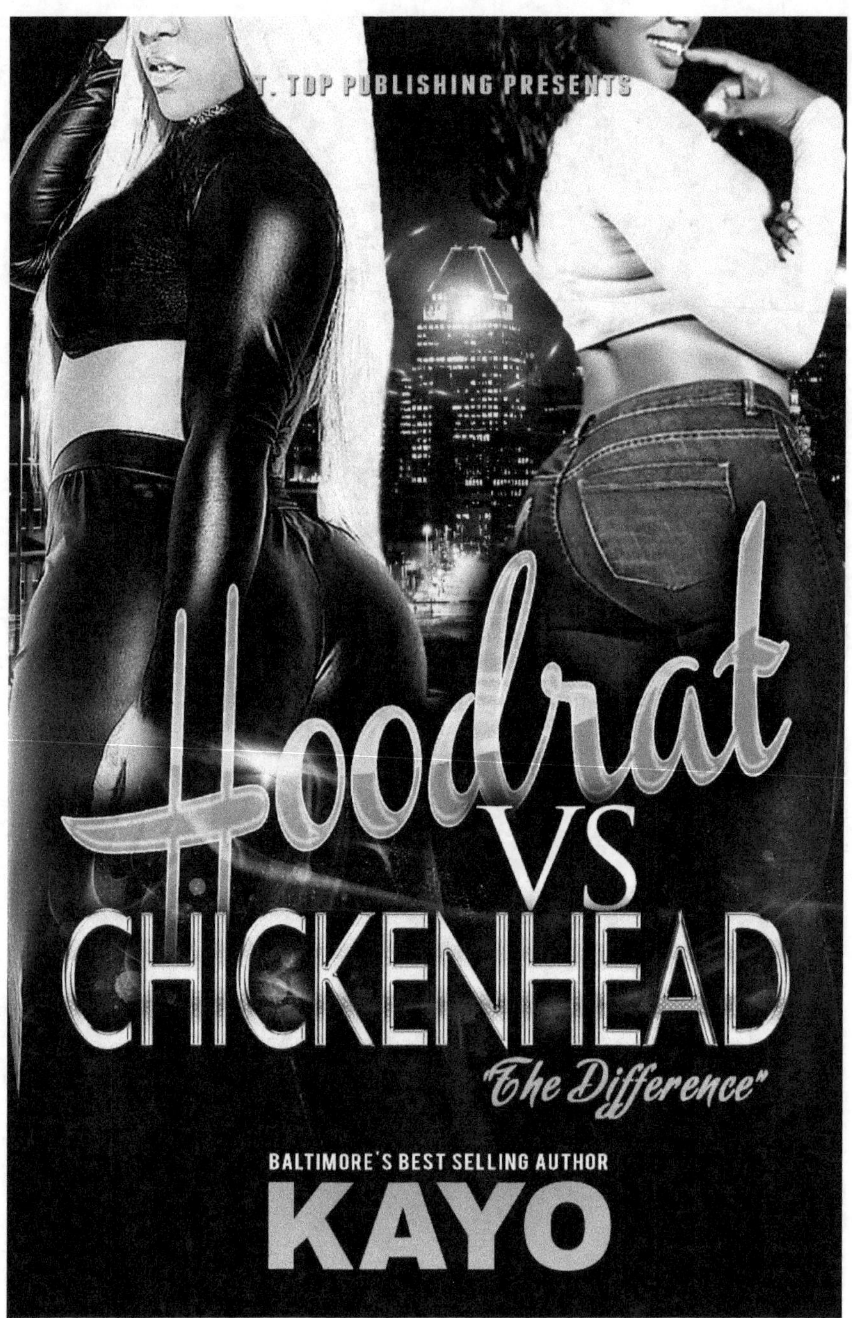
T. TOP PUBLISHING PRESENTS
Hoodrat
VS
CHICKENHEAD
"The Difference"
BALTIMORE'S BEST SELLING AUTHOR
KAYO
T. TOP PUBLISHING PRESENTS

COMING

SOON

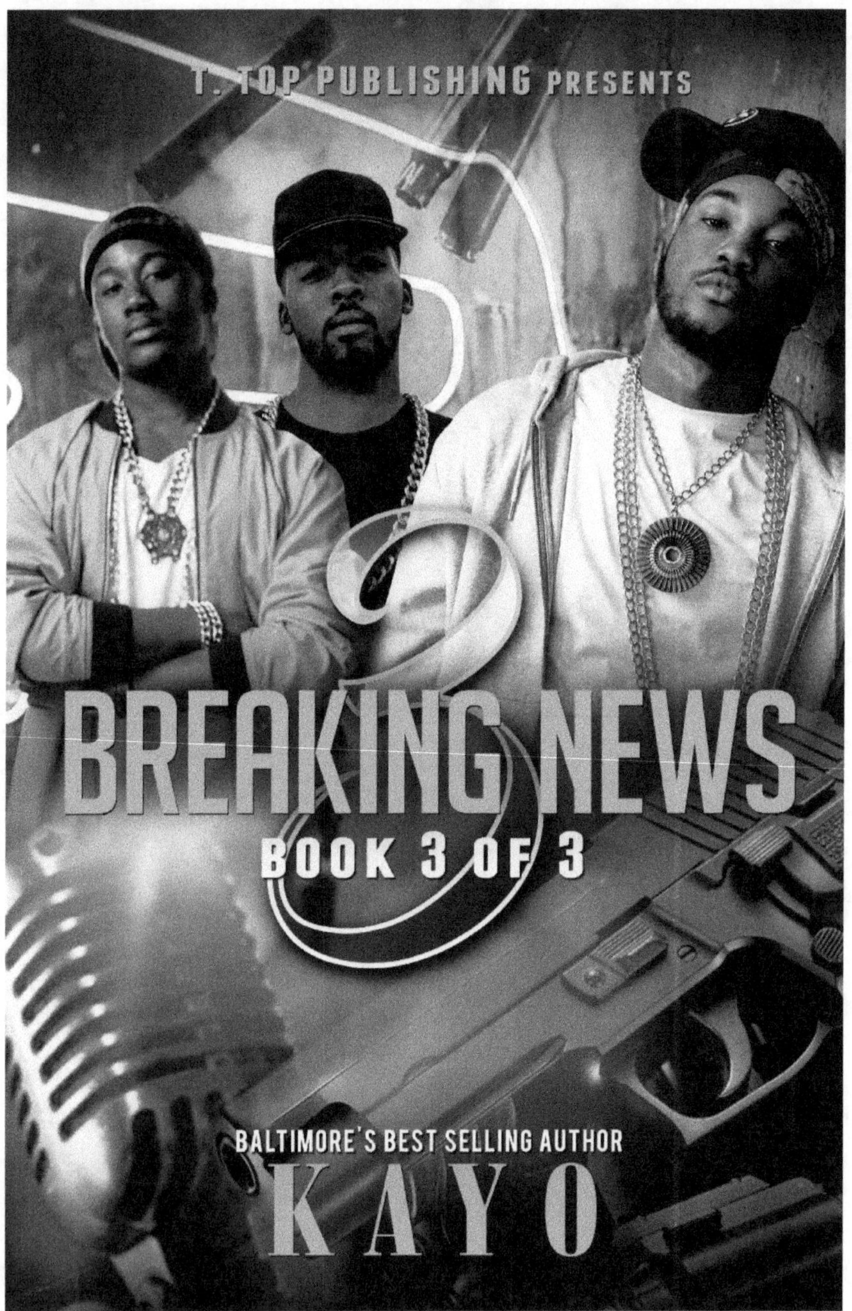
T. TOP PUBLISHING PRESENTS
BREAKING NEWS
BOOK 3 OF 3
BALTIMORE'S BEST SELLING AUTHOR
KAYO

T. TOP PUBLISHING PRESENTS
CITY OF GODZ
KILLER SEASON
BALTIMORE'S BEST SELLING AUTHOR
KAYO

T. TOP PUBLISHING PRESENTS
FRIENEMIES
How It All Began
BOOK 5 OF 10
5
BALTIMORE'S BEST SELLING AUTHOR
KAYO

T. TOP PUBLISHING PRESENTS
FRIENEMIES
Goon Affiliated
6
BOOK 6 OF 10
BALTIMORE'S BEST SELLING AUTHOR
KAYO

T. TOP PUBLISHING PRESENTS
FOURS
N.A.S.
Niggas Ain't Shit
'A STORY FOR ALL'
BALTIMORE'S BEST SELLING AUTHOR
KAYO

T. TOP PUBLISHING PRESENTS
THA TWINZ
REALLY WITH THE SHITS
BOOK 1 OF 2
BALTIMORE
POLICE
BALTIMORE'S BEST SELLING AUTHOR
KAYO

T. TOP PUBLISHING PRESENTS
THA TWINZ
II
FAMILY SECRETS
BOOK 2
BALTIMORE'S BEST SELLING AUTHOR
KAYO